THE ALPINE COACH

Clare Dubeque was pretty near penniless when she received an offer of employment from the Principessa Visconti. With her parents executed on the guillotine and her fiancé rapidly losing interest when he discovered her dowry had gone, Clare was prepared to do almost anything to keep herself alive.

But the kidnapping of a child from the Hotel Dieu, the outwitting of a brave but wounded Napoleonic officer, and a wild chase across Europe, culminating in a nightmare Alpine crossing, was to change Clare's life forever.

The Alpine Coach

Virginia Coffman

CORGI BOOKS

THE ALPINE COACH

A CORGI BOOK 0 552 99174 0

First published in the U.S.A. by Dell Publishing Co. Inc.

First British Edition published by Souvenir Press Ltd.

PRINTING HISTORY

Souvenir Press edition published 1980
Corgi edition published 1986

This book is set in 12/13 English Times

Corgi Books are published by Transworld Publishers Ltd.,
Century House, 61–63 Uxbridge Road, Ealing,
London W5 5SA, in Australia by Transworld Publishers
(Aust.) Pty. Ltd., 26 Harley Crescent, Condell Park, NSW
2200, and in New Zealand by Transworld Publishers (N.Z.)
Ltd., Cnr. Moselle and Waipareira Avenues, Henderson,
Auckland.

Made and printed in Great Britain by the
Guernsey Press Co. Ltd., Guernsey, Channel Islands.

Acknowledgements

In checking my backgrounds and topography, I am particularly indebted to the following:

Napoleon and Paris, by Maurice Guerrini (Walker)

Paris Through the Ages, by Pierre Couperie (Braziller), for excellent map work

The Grand Tour, by Christopher Hibbert (Putnam)

Guillotine in the Wings and *My Revolution,* by Alex Karmel (McGraw-Hill)

Boswell's *The Grand Tour*

Paris, The Turbulent City, by André Castelot (Barrie & Rockliff)

Travels in France, by Arthur Young

Illustrated History of Paris and Parisians, by Robert Laffont et al. (Doubleday)

Daily Life in the French Revolution and *Daily Life in France Under Napoleon,* by Jean Robiquet (Macmillan)

CHAPTER ONE

SEARCHING for the words in which to break off my betrothal, I had been chewing thoughtfully on the frayed goose quill of my pen for several minutes before I caught myself at this nervous habit and set the pen back in its standish. The sputtering pen had spotted the folds of my skirt. Since I was not very rich in clothing or, indeed, in anything else, I stood up hastily, tried to brush the stain away and was properly served for my carelessness when this merely set the stain. My cherry-striped silk gown was one of three that remained to me, and though frequently mended, had served me well during the past two years. But its loss would be a small matter in view of the problem of this letter.

'My very dear Paul,' I had begun, and after a little thought, struck out the 'very'. 'You are in Geneva. I am in Paris. Although France is in excellent communication with the Swiss cantons, you find it difficult to send your all too infrequent letters to me. You act so strangely. Have you become one more of France's enemies? I am persuaded I would love you though you were a traitor, but I believe you would prefer your freedom from me. Otherwise, you would find the time and inclination to write to me more often than every three months. We have led separate lives since you chose to become affiliated with banking circles in Geneva. The letters you do write to me are invariably full of your interest in banking and patronesses, obtaining new

9

backing, and the like. These are not the letters of a man who is at all anxious to return to France. Do you not believe we should now consider ending our betrothal?'

The breakoff of a betrothal was a painful and unsettling affair in any circumstances. However, in my heart, I had always known Paul Vallier cared more about making a financial success than he cared about me, Clare Dubeque. My parents had been good revolutionaries in spite of their membership in the small, moneyed middle class before the Revolution, but their death on the guillotine and the confiscation of most of my inheritance must have been a shock to Paul. Unfortunately, he had asked me to marry him only two months before my parents' arrest, which was ill-timed on his part, but he could not have guessed my inheritance would be withheld from me.

All that was nearly six years past, in 1794, and now I was twenty-three. Paul Vallier had been my broad-shouldered, noble ideal when I was seventeen, and I told myself I was unlikely ever to marry if I could not have him; for there could not be another like him, not at this age, when I was very nearly on the shelf.

I was still trying to find words which would not betray my deep sense of loss and estrangement from life at the breaking of the engagement. I had clung to him in my mind so desperately after the death of my parents! But now the winter sun poured down through the little Left Bank street, and it was impossible to concentrate on grim matters with that gaudy light crossing the miniature balcony outside my window.

It was time I gained a little composure and cheerfulness from that afternoon light. I pushed my chair back from the mahogany tilt-top table which served me as a desk and also for dining, on the infrequent occasions when I ate in my room or had my meals sent up from the little café in the nearby Rue de la Harpe. It was still considered a mark of the effete aristocrat to dine alone in one's lodgings. But the worst days of the Revolutionary Terror of 1794 were long since past, and having survived the agonies of the Republic's birth, I was beginning to share the French pride in our recovery from the dreadful *Law of Suspects* which had orphaned me.

I opened the window and stepped out on the tiny balcony, wondering how Paul could have given up all this: the narrow, busy streets with their medieval buildings tumbling toward each other, the excited anticipation of a new century that General Bonaparte, now First Consul, had brought to a country long pressed on all sides by the tyrants of Europe. The days of famine were gone now; order had returned, and some prosperity. People cared about the small things of life again. They were preparing for a gay Christmas and New Year, one of the first in a dozen years. But then, this was the threshold of a new century.

And the sun was shining. Pouring through the alleys and casting in sharp, shadowed relief the domes of the many churches now filling with pre-Christmas worshippers who would not have dared to worship publicly only five years before. I stepped farther out, leaned over the wrought iron rail, and caught a glimpse of the glittering Seine: first the Pont Neuf, and then beyond, the busy little rowboat-ferries that carried the traffic back and forth from the Right Bank and the Île de la Cité to the less fashionable, but no less busy, Left Bank.

As always, I was stimulated by that view of Paris' lifeline, and I wondered how Paul could find a career in the Swiss cantons to compensate him for its loss. Unless, of course, he remained in Switzerland only to avoid me. But wouldn't it be much simpler for him merely to ask for a release from our betrothal? Why did he keep writing, if only infrequently, when it was obvious that he no longer loved me, if indeed he ever had. I assured myself proudly that he would have no difficulty in obtaining his release.

I had managed to work up both anger and determination. I stepped back into my room, already composing the haughty lines that would cut him out of my quiet and uneventful life. It was not a life I sought. I was as romantic as the next young woman. But I assured myself firmly that I would obtain a post of some sort, seamstress perhaps – heaven knows I had enough practice in mending things – and resign myself to a sterile spinsterhood. There were worse fates.

I had scarcely reached for the pen again when an unexpected visitor scratched on my door. Even now, after more than five years, there was often a second when the old alarm signalled in my head: *it is Prosecutor Tinville's men, come to escort you to the Conciergerie.* It was how they had come for my parents.

'Yes. Who is there?' I asked, going to the door where I waited, my fingers flexing nervously, for the answer. It was soon forthcoming. Sylvie Vallier, who would have been my sister-in-law, called out in the light, silvery voice that always promised a friendship which remained elusive. 'Sylvie, chérie. Do come. I have the most marvellous post for you. You will not credit it. Too delicious!'

Our friendship was one of those useful affairs between people who find it necessary to present a united front before a new and sometimes hostile world. I pulled the door open and she came in, a vision of sparkling gold, from the Grecian bandeau and wispy curls to the sandals that revealed bare toes which, due to the condition of the alleys on both river banks, were far from clean. I looked up quickly, embarrassed at having noticed a matter which was not properly my concern. It was only the new fashion ushered in by people like Josephine Bonaparte's friend, Thérèse Tallien. I sometimes thought I would like to follow the fashion of sandals and bare feet – clean, I hoped! – if I were prosperous and able to have such daring gowns made for me. And it was daring, for the fashionable women of Paris had begun to dampen their thin muslin gowns in order to make them cling to an astonishing variety of shapes. This style, of course, was likely to earn a disgusted remark from First Consul Bonaparte, but what could he do when his enchanting wife led the pack?

Sylvie and I embraced, and I admired the beautiful arrangement of her hair, which was a particular buttery blonde that perfectly complemented her pale blue eyes. She had Paul's complexion. She adjusted her silk shawl and then grasped my shoulders excitedly. She was given to enthusiastic beginnings.

'But Clare, how foolish of you not to do as much with that splendid hair of yours! Much thicker than mine and if you were to tint it – well, I promise you, the *merveilleuses* would gnash their teeth with jealousy. Such a mousy brown! No matter. You will do very well for the post, perhaps even better than if you had done something with your assets. You are not the sort who needs embellishment, not with your eyes. Come, tell me, what do you think of my new ring? From Citizen Barras' aide himself.'

I glanced at her hands but she stamped her right foot impatiently.

'No, no, stupide! My toe. The ring on my big toe. Rings on the feet are all the crack this month. Mine is a pearl.'

Regrettably, the pristine, pink-glowing pearl only called attention to the matter of her feet. I said hastily that the stone was breathtaking as, indeed, it was, and asked, 'What is all this about a post? You may believe I should be grateful for a position of any kind.'

'Just so! And you shall have it. You have but to agree. How pretty you look in your red stripes!'

'Cherry.'

'Yes, precisely. Its quaintness suits you, Clare.' I wrinkled my nose at this but she bubbled on. 'It has a kind of quiet strength, and that is very much to the purpose, as you shall see. Let me find your shawl.'

'No, wait. Where are we going? If this is one of your jokes! I must find a position, Sylvie. I really must. It is urgent, so I haven't time to wander about the cafés at teatime.'

Tea was excessively English, and the English were our enemies, but Paris continued to drink tea, or sometimes wine, at this hour of late sunset. It was a civilised tradition, and when Sylvie brusquely dismissed my half-hearted protest, I made no further objections but changed to some attractive walking slippers and draped around my shoulders my best silver-threaded shawl, which matched the silver silk between the narrow stripes of my gown. If I held the scarf's folds correctly, I would be able to conceal the ink stain. I felt much more cheerful now, although I hadn't the least notion of where we were going or what this was all about.

It was a trifle curious because Sylvie rarely spread favours about. I had been fooled very often by her pose of easy, charming helpfulness. It invariably ended in my doing something she found too unpleasant, like the time she mislaid her identity papers and sent me off to the local Section Committee to inquire about the penalties. Actually, I had been very frightened, but anxious to oblige Paul's sister in any way possible. A wretched creature I must have seemed when I appeared before the huge, pockmarked man standing beside the section leader's desk, and I know he guessed my alarm. His voice made me jump. I had never heard such reverberating tones in a small room, and I knew he must have swayed great masses of his fellow citizens. But his words and his manner soothed and reassured me. I was always to remember the sad little curve in his smile as he remarked to the black-plumed section leader, 'Are we destined now to eat up our children as well?' And by this special attention to me, he had sent me home over the cobblestones as if walking on air.

Less than three weeks later Citizen Georges Danton rode through the narrow, ancient Rue St Honoré, giving courage to his companions as he had cheered me, on his way to the guillotine. Not until Citizen Bonaparte had we known another man who could lead us up from the abyss.

'Where are we going tonight?' I asked Sylvie. 'I had rather be home in my lodgings before dark. This neighbourhood isn't the safest in the world.'

'Chérie, you need never return to the Latin Quarter if you succeed in a little scheme they—we have in mind.'

We were clicking down the narrow, turning stairs together, and I asked again what the post might be. But as we reached the street below, already plunged into blue-dark by the tumbled old buildings that framed the street, a crowd briefly blocked our way. They had gathered around a glazier knocked down in a collision with an Auvergnat water-seller, going home after his profitable day selling reasonably pure water which we sadly lacked. The big sheet of glass attached to the glazier's back had been shattered into hundreds of pieces, and the crowd was divided between a belief in the young Auvergnat's guilt and a less popular theory that the glazier had been clumsy. It was a minor tragedy, but part of the Paris scene, and I wondered again if Paul, my betrothed, ever missed the vivid, exciting daily life in the city of his birth. Apparently not. And he certainly didn't miss me!

I gave up the attempt to find out where we were going. I was desperate to accept any sort of post that would make it possible to enjoy one good meal a day besides the watered wine and biscuit that served for my breakfast. My suppers had gradually become scarcely more than repetitions of breakfast.

When we reached the crowded expanse of the Place St Michel, now called the Place Michel, Sylvie astonished me by snapping her fingers to summon an ancient fiacre drawn by an exceedingly hairy horse.

'We shall ride in great style,' she announced. 'I want to impress Thérèse with the fact that we do not need her offer, or the fortune of the Viscontis. Only when we do not need money are we offered a profitable bargain, my dear.'

'What in heaven's name have the Viscontis to say to anything?' I asked as we got into the fiacre, but Sylvie merely waved me to silence and gestured toward the grizzled coachman whose pointed ears were clearly open to any bits of gossip he might overhear. So I sat beside Sylvie while we rattled over the cobblestones in style, baffled by this mysterious reference to one of the most historic and distinguished families in northern Italy. Perhaps one of the Viscontis was visiting Paris at this moment and needed a seamstress. It would not be too surprising. Since General Bonaparte had freed northern Italy from the oppression of its Austrian masters, many Italians had sought success and fame in Paris. At all events, the name itself was promising.

We rattled through the Quarter, across the bridge,

and into the centre of the Île de la Cité with its endless medieval warrens and passages whose origin went back to the ninth century. Sylvie and I were obviously thinking the same thing, that these sinister, dark passages might hide a dozen assassins at this very moment. She looked back in disgust at the dreaded Conciergerie with its round towers, less than a square to the west of us.

'Dreadful district. Clare, why must you live on the Left Bank so I am forced to pass these hideous old wrecks?'

'Money, or lack of it, might be one reason,' I reminded her drily. But she had received her cue and rushed on.

'That shall be mended. Do you like children?'

'Not particularly.'

'Oh, come, Clare!'

'I like people. Some of them. And children are people.'

She sighed. 'You are in one of your contrary fits. Well, no matter. You will do, I believe.'

After this cryptic remark she said no more, and as we reached the great, grey hulk of the Louvre, I found we were going to Sylvie's own charming little apartment whose rental was paid by Citizen Barras himself, although an occasional bauble of value was furnished by some lesser light in her interesting and always profitable life.

'Please tell me what this is about,' I begged her finally. 'Is it a post with these Viscontis? Are they in Paris? My Italian is shockingly bad, but I am quick at study. I could communicate, I am certain.'

She giggled. 'So much will not be necessary. It is important only that you not become travel-sick. But for such a slim creature you have always had an admirable constitution. And then, too, it will enable you to travel near that laggard brother of mine. In fact, Paul was the first to suggest it.'

'Paul! He wants to see me?' I could scarcely credit it. I was very much excited by the news and could not hide my elation from Sylvie. I didn't want her to guess how much it meant to me to feel loved again.

Sylvie's lodgings were in the Rue St Honoré, not far from the Tuileries, which were now being refurbished. We had just missed the nightly review of the troops outside the Tuileries in the Carrousel Court, but I was too excited to care. I began to picture myself rushing up the five flights of stairs in my lodgings, reaching for the unfinished letter to Paul, and tearing it up. If Sylvie should be right, and I might fit the position offered, then I would earn enough to support myself even if Paul no longer wished to marry me. Best of all, I would be able to meet Paul directly, face to face, and discover whether he cared for me or had ever cared. It was better to know, one way or the other.

Sylvie's ancient lodging house was within a few doors of that in which Citizen Robespierre had lived with the Duplay family six years ago, but there the resemblance between the lodgings ended. There was none of Robespierre's austerity about the rooms leased by Sylvie Vallier-Beaupré-Anstice. Each of her brief marriages had helped her to accumulate the elegant furnishings of the salon and bedroom on the third floor of the building. I enjoyed visiting Sylvie and her splendour, but I never felt quite comfortable with her friends, who were all members of the sardonic, cutting *merveilleuse* set, people who would do anything for a joke or a profit. Only Citizeness Bonaparte had ever seemed to genuinely like people. But whispers had it that the lady was overfond of cuckolding the husband who adored her. It seemed to me that if I were married to a man who loved me, I would not act as . . .

But then, I wasn't Josephine Bonaparte. And I was not one of her set.

Sylvie and I climbed the stairs to be met by her pretty, raven-haired maid, Mirienne, who had been a soubrette at the Comédie Française and still seemed to be playing the part.

'Ah! Citizeness Sylvie! You are just in time. She is waiting for you. With such a very odd little man. Quite frightening. They do make me excessively nervous.'

'*Nom de Dieu*! I am late. I knew it would be so. If this matter fails – Never mind. Come, Clare.'

I needed no second invitation. A trifle breathless, we hurried into the narrow foyer and then, recovering our dignity, we walked into Sylvie's beautifully appointed salon. I saw at once why the maid had been so unnerved. Seated stiffly on the straw satin sofa across the room was an old woman, extraordinarily wrinkled, but wearing her finery as though it were her own young, perfectly fitted flesh. Her skirts were as full as mine, and worn over petticoats in a fashion now several years behind the times. Over her gown she wore a velvet pelisse heavily trimmed with rich white fur, with a bonnet to match. She stared at me for a long and uncomfortable moment.

'You! Come here.'

I was so surprised at her discourtesy that I obeyed her, and belatedly noticed a wizened little man seated far from the long windows and hence in shadow. He was not old, probably in his thirties, but his sallow face had a pinched look, emphasised by a thin-lipped mouth like a slash. His small-eyed gaze kept darting around from one to the other of us, but it was clear he took his orders from the wrinkled old lady.

'Do you know me?' the old woman asked me sharply.

I had recovered my poise by now and, careful not to curtsey, managed to say coolly, 'No, Citizeness. I have not had the honour. And do you know me, by chance?'

Sylvie gasped at what she probably took to be my effrontery but the old woman snorted, not entirely in anger, I thought.

'Well said. As it happens, I do know you, Mademoiselle Dubeque, at least by reputation. Tell me now, before we proceed. I must know. Are you brave?'

'Tolerably so, Citizeness,' I said, not mincing words.

She winced at the revolutionary title but looked hard at me. 'When I say brave, I mean, are you capable of genuine courage? Against a true horror?'

At last she had found me speechless.

CHAPTER TWO

EVERYONE was staring at mè, even Sylvie who must certainly have known the subject of the old lady's threatening remark.

'Now, child, let me present myself, since the cat seems to have seized Madame Vallier's tongue. I am the Principessa Visconti. Of Milano, naturally.'

'Naturally, Citizeness. Perhaps you had forgotten we no longer recognise titles in the Republic. But I believe you mentioned a post which requires courage? Are there other requirements?'

The princess nodded. 'To the point. I like that. Yes, there are other requirements. But there is danger, both to yourself and especially to your charge.'

'My charge?'

'Yes. Did not this tiresome Sylvie explain? My granddaughter's child. I was especially informed that you adore children. This is true, is it not?'

'No, Citizeness. It is not true.'

The sinister little man started to get up, and Sylvie cried in disgust, 'Clare! Need you be so frank?'

Unexpectedly, the princess was undisturbed. She waved to her unpleasant henchman, who scrambled back onto his hard, ladder-back chair.

'I see no reason why there should by hypocrisy in all this. I have always favoured frankness. Do come and sit down here where I can see you. Sylvie, bring in the candles. Or tell that addlepated

21

maid to make herself useful.' Both of us obeyed her, while I wondered at the hints of 'terror' and 'courage' and a journey. These hints were tantalising enough, as she must know, to hold me silent while the principessa began to instruct me.

'There is an estate in Lombardy, the largest estate of the Viscontis of Milano, whose heiress, if she lives, is a child of twelve named – ' she made a face indicative of disgust ' – Linette Redon. So plebeian! But my husband's granddaughter by his first marriage was a free-thinker. She met this wretched Marius Redon while visiting a schoolmate in Paris a year or two before the Revolution spread its cancer over Europe.' She shrugged. 'But that is all by the way. The important thing is that my husband's granddaughter died of a fever several years ago, leaving the child in the hands of the husband, this wretched Marius Redon, some sort of officer in the army of Bonaparte. Then my husband, the Principe Gianmaria Visconti, died. And a good half of the estate will be Linette's, although an uncle of the child, Bernardo Visconti, a singularly ill-favoured creature, is determined that he and Redon shall control the child's fortune. It seems they have both been among Bonaparte's rag-tag army, and are old comrades. I need not tell you the danger, if Linette and her father die before she reaches her majority. Bernardo will have it all. You understand me now?'

Vaguely, I began to see a pattern in all this Visconti history, but not necessarily the pattern she wove for me so obligingly. 'And you intend to return to Milano now with the child, this Linette Redon?'

'That is what Bernardo expects me to do. And I have no doubt his agents are watching my movements carefully at this moment, through some spy or other.'

It was difficult to keep from looking over one's shoulder at this news. I only just managed to remain collected.

'But what of the child's father? Will he not protect her on this journey to Milano to claim the estate?'

'He might, if he were not himself a dying man. Some damage to the lungs during the Egyptian campaigns, I believe. In any event, he is a patient in that dreadful hospital of yours here in Paris. The Hôtel Dieu, I believe it is called.' She shuddered, as well she might. It was a place of death. Even I knew it, although I had never been within its doors. 'An impossible man. Will not give up the child. And in his condition! He will not even see me.'

'But Madame,' I began, forgetting the revolutionary title and interested in her problem in spite of myself, 'what is to prevent the child's uncle, this Bernardo, from killing young Linette after she reaches your estates in Milano?'

'There will be no reason, no profit. We shall have it all arranged by our bankers so that he may not profit, no matter what becomes of the girl.'

From her tone I knew she believed this, true or not.

'I am afraid I have not understood you, Citizeness,' I said after a curiously pregnant silence. 'If this Marius Redon won't surrender his child to you, how can I be of assistance? What inducement – that is to say, how is this unfortunate man to be induced to part with her?' I looked at their faces and began to burn with contempt. My voice sounded harder to my own ears as I added, 'Or are you waiting to·hear of the young man's death? After which, I daresay, it will be simple enough for you to snatch his daughter away?'

Sylvie gave out an irritating titter of a laugh and then hastily slapped her palm over her mouth, but the princess was not amused. There was a spark in her eyes, distinctly anger. Her thin, pallid lips pursed together like the top of a lady's reticule with the draw-strings tightly drawn.

'I fear you misunderstand, Mademoiselle. I have no intention of snatching Marius Redon's daughter from a man on his deathbed.' She paused like an actress skilled in her timing. I caught my breath. I guessed the answer before she added, with a return of the sardonic humour I had suspected from the first, 'No. Not I. In my position it would not be fitting. It is you who will . . . persuade Monsieur Redon.'

'I? Are you mad? What possible influence could I have upon a poor, suffering creature whose child I want to steal?'

The sharp-faced little man clicked the heels of his boots together.

'She is in the right of it, you know.'

I was surprised at his tone, almost one of equality with the old lady; yet she did not appear surprised. But of one thing I was certain: all his actions were dependent upon her command.

As if she and I were alone in the room, the princess turned to me, took my hand in her rough, dry fingers, and gazed at me with watery but penetrating eyes. There was something vaguely alarming about her; but she had behaved with the manner, even the appalling rudeness of the true aristocrat, as my mother had described them.

'I am very taken with you, my child. You have a certain acerbic quality and a fine strength that will serve you well. And there is honesty in your face, your voice. I am persuaded these qualities may be useful.'

To whom? I wondered, but said nothing. My so-called honesty, my 'fine' strength had done little for me to this date. I had even lost my betrothed. Or had I?

'Citizeness, are you acquainted with Colonel Paul Vallier?'

She blinked, but answered brightly, 'How else could I have known of your excellent qualities? Young Vallier was good enough to mention you when we discussed banking matters in Geneva. A most fortunate meeting. We talked of Paris – I knew it well as a girl at the court of the late king's father – and I mentioned my difficulty in reaching my granddaughter's child. The stubborn, unyielding determination of the young father who, to all accounts, will be dead within a matter of months.'

Sylvie put in, obviously puzzled by such conduct, 'But doesn't he know his child will receive a fortune? How can he be so selfish?'

I said nothing. I did not know Marius Redon or his attitude towards his late wife's people, but I thought it probable that he was simply afraid for his daughter's life. Or even that in his present condition, she was his only comfort. I felt maudlin in considering such a possibility.

'A selfish beast, my dear Sylvie. Aptly put. Our young friend here, Mademoiselle Dubeque, may be just the person to deal with him. He will believe her. He must, if he is human at all.'

'I should not wish to think I was separating a dying man from his daughter,' I put in, trying not to sound as dogged and as 'acerbically' honest as she pretended to find me. 'Perhaps it would be wiser to wait, after all.'

Wait for the death of Linette Redon's young father? A morbid thought, and I wished I had not proposed it. Sylvie Vallier looked at me admiringly.

'You really can be hard, can't you? That had quite a cruel edge to it.'

But the old princess sent an angry glance in her direction. 'Be silent if you cannot be helpful, you chatterbox!' She continued in the most buttery tone to me, 'My dear, it will not serve. The child is daily, and I might say nightly, menaced. Only two days ago she became deathly ill from tainted fish, I am told. Everyone at that old hospital denies it, but a kitchen wench declared that a very ill-favoured fellow was hanging about Linette's dinner plate before the child ate.'

'You mean that poor child lives in a place like the Hôtel Dieu with all those dying people?' I asked incredulously. My revulsion at the idea of separating father and daughter had begun to fade. The sooner young Linette was removed from such an atmosphere, the better.

The princess brightened at my indignant question and pointed out in triumph, 'You see now why it is urgent.'

'Indeed, yes, I agree. If only there were some way to spare the wretched father any more pain and grief.'

The princess shrugged her bony shoulders. '*He* would be better off if someone took a knife to him one of these dark nights, to end his sufferings, as I suppose he must suffer. Marius Redon has never considered my feelings, nor even the fact that my sector of the family can protect his daughter far better from Bernardo and his family than a man who is dying.'

'Must we talk of knives and killings?' Sylvie asked, echoing my own silent complaint. 'It should be a simple matter if Clare does her work well. She can be very persuasive. Paul always said so.'

It was a curious thing for Paul to have said about me. He might have called me dear or sweet, or even superfluous to his life in the Swiss cantons, but persuasive? I had not even been able to persuade him to marry me in five years. I laughed and they all stared at me. I had startled them. The maid had set a pair of delicate cups and saucers on the table

26

within reach of the princess and me. I did not reach for the tea too eagerly, nor for the wafers beside Sylvie's exquisite china, which she had acquired from the sale of Madame du Barry's pavilion outside Paris.

I wanted the wafers and tea almost desperately. They would form a very large portion of my supper that night, but I would not, for worlds, have let the princess guess how empty my purse was. She would not be above using financial pressures to bring me into her service. After the others had begun to drink, I took up my own cup with what I hoped was a certain casualness.

How good it tasted! There was a faint flavour of oranges in it. I drank and dreamed of spending an hour every day at this delightful pastime. But only if I accepted the rather dubious post offered me. Everyone seemed to expect me to accept eagerly, but it still appeared to me that the princess could defend her great-granddaughter better than I.

'Well? Well?' the princess barked suddenly.

'I don't know just what I am – I mean what I would be – expected to do. Could you not restore her to her estate with stronger guardians, Citizeness Visconti?'

'Foolish child! Bernardo would be watching me at all points, I have no doubt. I intend to lead him in quite a different direction. I shall be the decoy.'

Sylvie cried out with great impatience.

'How can you be so dense, Clare? You are to take Linette Redon from Paris to Milano, while the princess leads her enemies by private coach. There is nothing very difficult about your work.'

'Don't lie,' the princess admonished Sylvie. 'It is not simple, of course. First you must persuade that impossible young man that Linette will be safe with you. You will then take the child to the public

Accommodation Coach which departs for Lyon from the Hôtel de Sens at some ungodly hour.'

'Lyon,' I echoed, dazed by this rapid recitation.

'Precisely. In Lyon, you will escort Linette to the Alpine Coach. This is heavier, more durable. It will take you over Mont Cenis Pass. Treacherous, I will allow, but it is done every week. However, I do not mince words. It is a rough journey, but rougher on the carcass of a bony old female like myself.'

I smiled at her description and Sylvie tittered. Outside the long windows, night had plunged the narrow street below into a stygian dark scarcely relieved by the flickering lanterns that were being hoisted into place. It looked as though I must return home in darkness, after all, not a happy thought.

I was perfectly aware that they all expected a definite answer which I could not, in conscience, give them.

Sylvie spoke for all of them. 'Clare, you are really the outside of enough! You know quite well you are going to accept Her Highness' very generous offer. Why do you not say so? You will oblige—'

'Wait!' The Principessa Visconti held up one hand. 'We have not assured Mademoiselle Dubeque of our very material gratitude.' I was amused at her use of the royal 'we.' She certainly didn't expect Sylvie to join in paying me. She was about to explain when there were sounds on the stairs outside the salon's mirrored foyer.

Sylvie excitedly pushed Mirienne toward the door and I noted that the ferret-faced man was instantly alert.

'I know that step,' Sylvie cried. 'Thérèse is here. We are going to walk in the Palais Royal. Oh! I shouldn't say "royal." We shall pretend to be prostitutes and then see the soldiers' faces when they pursue us and learn our identities.'

'*Per Dio*!' murmured the princess, rolling her eyes to the high, gilded ceiling. 'And what does the lady's husband say to such pranks?'

'Tallien? Pooh! Who cares about him? He saved us from Robespierre, but he has done absolutely nothing since. Mirienne, do open the door . . . chérie! No, no, no! You are just in time. Our tiresome conference is ended and dear Clare is going to brave the lion in the Hôtel Dieu.'

I started to object to this bold assumption but was silenced by the confusion when Sylvie ushered in the gorgeous creature whose potent charms as a prisoner in the Conciergerie had incited her lover to flout the deadly power of Robespierre five years before, and almost as a secondary issue, had brought an end to the Terror. Thérèse Cabarrus Tallien glittered in transparent flame-coloured silk which clung to her slightly thickening body, managing to reveal almost every line. The effect was wasted upon an audience chiefly made up of women.

The princess responded with a tight little smile of contempt. In a low aside, she remarked to me, 'A woman of some power and influence in Paris, I take it.'

'At one time. But I believe not in the last three or four years, since order has been restored to the government.'

'I am happy to hear it!' said the old lady tightly. Nevertheless, she managed to sit a little straighter and to hold out her hand. Thérèse responded with a slight bow as she touched the princess' fingers with her own. Turning to me, she tossed her thick hair in its elaborate Grecian curls. Her heavy-lidded eyes indicated she needed sleep, but there was no denying her voluptuous beauty.

'Ah! My dear Paul's affianced bride. Quaint and lovely. Exactly the sort who might succeed.'

The princess raised her chin.

'Am I to understand, Madame, that you are acquainted with the matter under discussion here?'

Thérèse shrugged, made a little moue in Sylvie's direction with her plum-coloured lips. 'Briefly. My friend Sylvie thought it might be helpful for me to busy myself with the administration of the Hôtel Dieu part of the arrangement. Nothing would suit me better, for you must know I adore that rogue. But it was not of the slightest use. He would not see me. Detestable, perverse creature!'

She had certainly left me far behind in her talk of Marius Redon, a man whom she adored, but who was detestable and perverse! And a dying man beside all else!

'She means –' Sylvie began uneasily, but was silenced by her own inability to explain.

The princess voiced her reaction without hesitation. 'Females act excessively stupid over men nowadays. In my time males were neither adorable nor detestable, although,' she added, apparently upon a vagrant memory of her own, 'they may have been perverse on occasion, I will allow. Now, Mademoiselle Dubeque, this matter of obtaining leave to remove the child and then of delivering her to my family in Milano will be worth, say, ten thousand assignats to you.'

'Say no,' Thérèse advised merrily. 'You know an assignat is not worth the paper it's printed on. Bonaparte threatens to create a Bank of France but you can scarcely wait for that. Ask for your pay in English pounds on some English company in Livorno. It is not so far from Milano. Then you can have it changed to French livres in Geneva on your return.'

Madame Thérèse was far from stupid and I took her advice as correct, but I explained again, 'I cannot agree to this matter until I know a good deal more about it, and certainly not until I have met Citizen Redon.'

'Aha!' Thérèse exclaimed. 'I do envy you, my girl. We used to find him quite challenging when he was in Paris between campaigns.'

'Challenging because he would never tumble you in his bed, Thérèse,' Sylvie put in.

'That too. I wonder how our new young recruit here will fare.'

Was the man dangerous even on his deathbed? I was conscious of a heat of embarrassment that probably showed itself in my cheeks but I got up, thanked Sylvie for her hospitality, and prepared to leave. The princess tried to hold me back by vainly groping for my fingers.

'What do you say, child? Say, two hundred pounds paid to you for the task. I will go so far as to pay you fifty pounds upon account, before you leave this room, and another fifty when you accept.'

It was tempting, but I could not accept the offer without hopelessly compromising myself in the matter, and I was determined to make no irreversible move without the consent of the patient in the Hôtel Dieu.

'Forgive me if you please, Citizeness, but I cannot agree to any arrangement until we have the permission of the child's father.'

'Then gain that permission, Mademoiselle. Gain it. And at once. Tomorrow.' She allowed me to touch her hand when I curtseyed, then waved me away as she would have dismissed an importunate chambermaid.

I managed to walk calmly to the foyer. I did not want her to imagine she was rushing me away. Madame Thérèse had begun to chatter with the old lady but Sylvie was courteous enough to follow and bid me good night.

'Chérie, it is still early. Dark, I know, but early.

31

I used nearly my last sou to bring you over here. Otherwise I could help you to hire a carriage.'

'My dear Sylvie,' I reminded her a trifle tartly, 'I have walked all my life, and certainly I can walk to the Ferry at the Place de la Révolution, and I can walk home along the river bank from there.' Then I remembered. 'No, they are digging for Bonaparte's new quai. I'll take the Pont Neuf through the Île to the Place Michel.'

'Excellent. But don't linger on the Île. You know how it is, especially that dreadful slum around Notre Dame.' She laughed. 'I shouldn't like to be responsible for the rape or murder of my future sister.'

'Of course not. Good night.' Pulling my shawl more tightly around my throat, I went down the stairs. I was not precisely certain why I should be so angry with that group in her salon, including Sylvie herself. They had made me an offer. I need not accept it. Why lay the blame upon them?

I came out into the filthy street, knowing all the refuse would be swept away – if only temporarily – by the morning sweepers, but meanwhile I walked with care. The worst obstacles were the carriages and the horses with their flying manes. All the elegant females and every male of any consequence were dashing off to cafés for dinner parties. Prosperity seemed to be everywhere and I began to tell myself I was a fool not to have accepted the princess' offer upon the instant, along with her fifty pounds paid over in French money. I was revolted at the thought of my being instrumental in depriving a dying man of his child. But even more important, I did not think I would like being in debt to the Principessa Visconti for any reason.

I walked rapidly the length of St Honoré as far as the prominent Café Régence. On a crowded corner near the Louvre Palace, two drunken but elegant young gentlemen assumed the worst about me but were dissuaded when I said coolly, 'You will find a much more likely pair a few steps behind me.'

This struck them as riotously amusing and they staggered off in the direction from which I had just come. I went on, cut through a dingy, crowded area of shacks and hovels beyond the Louvre to the great stone bridge. The water of the river glistened with the occasional reflection of a light from the littered and muddy shores. As I crossed to the Île de la Cité on my way to the Left Bank, I caught a glimpse of the enormous and ugly hospital, the Hôtel Dieu, that brooded over the Île in a sinister way, and suddenly I decided to visit the patient, Marius Redon, tonight, before I lost my courage.

CHAPTER THREE

I turned and walked rapidly along the river bank where workers, looking strange in their long revolutionary trousers, were busily digging another stone quai by lantern light. Someone whistled at me, a harmless whistle because the cheerful fellow was far below me in the river mud, so I smiled and hurried on. Although the air had been delightfully balmy, I found my shawl inadequate against the December night.

The Hôtel Dieu loomed like a square of darkness occupying the heart of the island near Notre Dame. Those who entered as patients seldom emerged except as corpses. It took a considerable effort to persuade myself to visit Marius Redon tonight, before I flatly refused the principessa's offer. I walked along under the cold, damp influence of those walls, seeking a light somewhere and a place of entry.

I finally reached the front entrance which was barred by a score of wretched people, mostly aged, complaining that they had no place else to sleep. I knew that if they were not permitted to spend the night in the hospital's halls they must make do along the river banks. I tried to banish their plight from my mind. I had matters of greater urgency that concerned me: the death, not of an ancient citizen, but of a young one, Marius Redon. Silently, I wished those unfortunate creatures the best of luck, and seeing a lantern flicker above a small door in the side of this huge medieval building, I knocked hard to rouse someone on the inside.

A dreadful-looking man in striped pantaloons and three different-sized jackets unbolted the little door with a great clank and scrape of rusty bolts.

'Ay! Roll in the creature. No room for another, but he'll never feel the crowding. Not him.'

'Not who?' I asked, perplexed and looking over my shoulder. 'I am alone.'

'What! Then what'll you be doing at this door? Surely you've a body there behind you some place that you are delivering for the shroud and all.'

I had to swallow hard before assuring him firmly that I was not the bearer of a corpse. I knew now that my choice of doors had been unfortunate. But I was inside the hospital now and there was no point in my retreating merely because I was repulsed by this necessary place.

'Forgive me for this intrusion, Citizen,' I began, 'but I wish to visit one of the patients above stairs. It is a matter of some importance.' I did not want to sound pompous, but I need not have concerned myself. My friend in this morgue, lighted by its curious red-hooded lanterns, had no ear for subtlety.

'Eh? It's not permitted, Citizeness. For fear you'll tell them that lies above stairs, their next step is down here in my gentle paws. Mine and the others.' He grinned, showing numerous empty spaces accentuated by sharp canine teeth, and he held up two enormous paws. To my horror the palms of his hands had a bloody glow. A second later I almost laughed, realising the lurid glow came from the swaying lantern suspended overhead.

'Oh, please, Citizen, if you could just make this one exception and show me the staircase! You see, I am not sure I will have the courage to enter again. And there is such a crowd.'

He glanced around the gloomy room where I

saw, piled against the far wall, at least a dozen of the cheapest coffins, mere boards thrown together with inadequate wooden pegs. On top of the coffins was a pile of home-spun cloth used for shrouds. I wondered if the coffins were filled, although I did not ask. The long, rough, deal table in the centre of the room was undoubtedly where the unfortunate dead of Paris were sewn into shrouds. I would dream about this place if I did not take care.

My friend had considered me from head to toe and, being finally moved by something about me, perhaps my persistence, he waved a brawny arm.

'This way, Citizen. Too bad, I say, too bad you'll not be one of my clients, so to speak. A prettier one never came rolling into my little workshop.'

My smile must have been a feeble one, but he seemed satisfied. His remark, of course, had been a compliment of no mean order. I went before him as he indicated, avoiding the coffins, and walked rapidly across the low-roofed room toward what my escort pointed out as the correct staircase.

He left me to make my own way up a flight of steps so narrow I had to draw in my single skirt and two petticoats, but even so, there was no escaping the dust and what must be years of dirt crusted over each step. I looked back once, but the Lord of the Charnel House remained at the bottom of the steps, looking up and grinning at me.

By the time I reached the first floor of the hospital, I was heartily ashamed of my concern over dust. What I saw in that central hall, with brief glimpses of dark side areas and alcoves, appeared to be a writhing, amorphous thing, groaning as one creature. Regretting my own gesture, but unable to avoid it, I covered my ears while I stood there, pushed and shoved first from one direction, then the other. Everyone was trying to find a place in which to squat, or to sit. There was no hope of stretching out to

37

sleep. They were piled against each other, these wretched remnants of a Paris that even the Revolution could not save from destitution. More than half of them were elderly, grizzled, crippled from diseases of the bone, doubtlessly worsened by having slept along the river banks many nights. But there were even children among them.

I knew then that I must get Linette Redon out of this place. Heaven knew what the result would be to her spirit if she became accustomed to such a life in death. She must grow up with decent, healthy surroundings. I would make Marius Redon understand that.

No attendant acknowledged me. Indeed, the few nurses I saw appeared to be of the sort I had heard about upon occasion. Two within my view were clearly drunken, staggering about, belligerent and cruel as they shoved a twisted old man into a corner where he lost his balance. Almost involuntarily, I reached out, but I was not quick enough. He tumbled over onto one hip and settled there, not moving, staring up at me with dazed eyes. I started to kneel before him but was jerked to my feet by a stout nurse whose breath reeked of strong spirits.

Five years ago, I thought, you would have been knitting below the guillotine in the Place de la Révolution. But I was discreet enough not to express this view by word or manner.

'Pardon, Citizeness,' I said, 'I do not mean to intrude, but I thought the old gentleman was confused.'

The woman's jowls shook with indignation. 'You talk like an aristo, my fine creature! There are fancy sick-houses for your kind. Go to Doctor Belhomme. Do not clutter our halls. We are too busy.'

I was distinctly in the wrong. These dreadful-looking women were doing far more to alleviate the suffering here than I. Somewhat chastened, I ventured earnestly, 'I am only calling to visit Citizen Marius Redon. Can you tell me how I may locate him? There seems to be some confusion.'

The place appeared to be a madhouse, and I understood now that these people were not patients, but unfortunates with no place to sleep. The nurse in her wine-stained gown raised her hand palm up between us. With a sigh, I took my last three sous out of my reticule, and dropped them into her palm. She grinned at once and tramped through that seething mass of misery with me following behind.

My first thought for these unhappy people was, I confess, a nervous desire to avoid them, but by the time my guide and I reached the steps at the end of the hall, I had decided it was time I stopped bemoaning the condition of these people and tried to furnish a little assistance myself. If I took young Linette Redon to safety in Milano, I would return and devote my time to assisting here in the hospital, if the authorities would have me.

When I reached the staircase, the stout nurse turned me over to a nun of one of the local nursing orders. Nuns were rarely seen since the Revolution, but this one had evidently sworn loyalty to the French Republic in defiance of the Papal order. Such sisters of healing were a great blessing to France in these days.

She was a tall woman with a lean, weathered face, and she bade me follow her up the stairs. When we were beyond the dreadful cacophony on the first floor, she looked back over her shoulder with no indication of approval or disapproval.

'So you are another calling upon Monsieur Redon.'

'Are there so many then, Sister?'

'Some. The First Consul has sent his aides to discover Monsieur's condition. He is most concerned and sent over some medication which, I am sorry to say, was not efficacious. But chiefly, Monsieur's visitors are female.'

It seemed an extraordinary thing that a dying man should still manage to attract females in general. But perhaps there was one in particular.

'I do not mean to have anyone suppose that I am visiting him from purely – ' I stopped, unable to express this to the nun who was now clearly amused.

'Carnal motives? No, Mademoiselle. They may have their carnal motives, but we are a trifle too public here for such things. I understand then that you are here on business of one sort or another. He is not to be hectored, you know. I will not allow that.'

I began to suspect that the good Sister was also moved by the young man, but I assured her that if Marius Redon refused to see me, that would be the end to my visit. I did not wish to force the issue. Besides, the more I heard about the young man, the less I liked the sound of him. It seemed to me that in his present condition he had best look to the salvation of his soul and not the entertaining of ladies with a 'carnal interest' in him. This was what my common sense told me. But unexpectedly, I discovered a sneaking sympathy for his refusal to give up a pleasure.

'I would not dream of hectoring him,' I assured her, as we walked carefully along the upper hall. It was not, strictly speaking, a corridor. It was simply an open space, an enormous room with little draped cubicles along one side and at the far end of the hall. The central hall was filled with patients. Many of these were elderly and, judging from their babblings, perhaps senile. There were far too few cots and almost half of the patients lay on dirty blankets upon the floor. I pitied them, the females on one side of a broad barricade, the males on the other, seeking their small pleasures by gossip with fellow inmates, or huddling to themselves. But the frightful thing to me was how many children, orphaned by the Revolution, lived and played among these poor crones. The children were virtually in rags but there seemed to be no depressing thoughts among those gamins with their young laughter, their contagious giggles.

'The severely injured and those in the last extremities are given the relative privacy of those curtained partitions. It is better for the morale of the living,' the sister informed me in her cool, practical tones.

I tried to exclude the irony from my own voice but I am certain I failed.

'As the living begin to die, they are removed to those cubicles?'

'Precisely,' the sister agreed, without inflection. 'But not the war-wounded, of course. They are being removed to the Invalides. We have learned much about the treatment of injuries as a result of the campaigns. This way. Do not step there. The poor fellow's leg is ulcerated. I fear it must go.'

I had just stepped over the old man's heavily bandaged leg when he called to my companion querulously. 'Sister Magdalen, my wine. Your promise! I had your promise.'

'Yes, yes, Jehan. A moment, if you please. I will just see to the wants of poor Monsieur Marius.'

The old man snorted. 'Poor Marius, indeed! He does very well for himself, this poor Marius and his females.'

I began to share the old man's feeling that Marius Redon sounded like a man who managed to have everything, even on his deathbed. Sister Magdalen went ahead of me to one of the curtained cubicles across the room. Hardly knowing what to expect, I followed her, and was much relieved to be greeted by a young girl's laughter from behind the heavy, moth-eaten crimson drape. Sister Magdalen pushed aside

41

the drape, stood a minute with her back to me, and then startled me by laughing.

'Excellent, Mademoiselle. Clearly, you win.' She moved into the tight little curtained room. I heard a male voice murmur something and Sister Magdalen, astonishingly, giggled.

'Monsieur,' she said crisply, recovering, 'we do not joke about such things. If the child wishes to embrace you before bidding you good night, I say nothing to that, but I am not here for the purpose. And I have a visitor.'

This time, I clearly heard Marius Redon speak in a voice of reasonable power. I was relieved that he was not too weak to talk, in any case.

'What sort of visitor?'

'A very presentable young female, Monsieur.'

'Oh, God, no! What have they sent to persuade me this time? A dazzler from the Comédie Française?'

'I leave you to judge, Monsieur.' The nun was stepping aside to make room for me when Marius Redon said unequivocally, 'No! Send her about her business.'

It was an awkward moment. I had already stepped inside the cubicle and was at the foot of his bed by the time he finished ordering me out. With all this talk of his females, I was prepared for a conceited fellow so popular with women that he had to order them away, but I was belatedly arrested by his remark, 'What have they sent to persuade me this time?' So it was not his charm but his possible use to the Principessa Visconti that caused this procession of female visitors!

The young man sitting up on his rickety cot looked ill enough in all conscience, judging by his sallow complexion, but his remarkably fine black eyes were so alive one forgot his condition. He wore an old army jacket over a shirt surprisingly white and clean for these surroundings. His thin but very active hands were still in position between those of a plain, snub-nosed girl of about twelve or thirteen, as both man and child had been trying to top each other's clasp on an old tree branch. It was evident that Mademoiselle Linette, as I supposed her to be, had won.

She looked around at me without too much interest, though not in an unfriendly way. I did not know whether to be flattered or not by the flicker of surprise in those long-lashed black eyes of the man I had come to see.

He was more attractive than I had imagined. Somehow, I had pictured Marius Redon as feeble, even skeletal. The lung injury had certainly left its imprint on his face, with the pallid mouth, and the darkness of his eyes set against the sallow flesh, but the curve of his lips was generous. Sensitive, too, I thought, and with a little more flesh upon those high-boned cheeks, he might easily have been considered handsome by women like Madame Thérèse Tallien who called him irresistible. The difference was that he looked like a man of taste, not a creature who would waste time with Thérèse and her coterie.

As he saw me, he blinked, giving himself a second to revise whatever he had started to say, while I, less clever about concealing my own feelings, behaved as stupidly as possible.

'Oh! I thought – Pardon, if you please. You are Citizen Redon?'

He smiled. Although not unpleasant, it was a singularly unreadable smile. 'Tell me, chérie, by what means did Her Highness acquire your services? Are you, by some incredible bad luck, indebted to the old harridan?'

I almost betrayed my amusement at his reading of the principessa's character and what I suspected to be her means of recruiting employees, but I managed to say coolly, 'Not thus far, but as I do not read palms, I cannot speak for the future.'

43

He surprised me by being definitely amused. 'At all events, you are more honest than the others. I mustn't keep you from those who need you, my love . . . '

Startled, I thought for an instant he was speaking to me, but Sister Magdalen nodded, chucked young Linette under her small, strong jaw, and very agreeably left the three of us alone. Or as alone as we could be, separated by a single curtain from the mass of noisy patients in the hall itself. It was only then that Marius Redon betrayed any signs of the fatal illness that had placed him in this alcove. He frowned, caught his breath, and his fingers flexed almost unconsciously, as if he had been pricked by a strong bodkin. His quick, flickering smile did not quite conceal the reaction.

'My neighbours become a bit lively just before the candles are snuffed,' he explained with a gesture of indifference.

'I hope the old man with the ulcerous leg receives the wine he was promised.'

'She means Jehan, that old man who spies on you when you have visitors,' the girl put in, speaking for the first time since I had entered the alcove.

Marius Redon said lightly, 'A tenderhearted damsel out of the principessa's stable. What other miracles shall we see tonight?'

I did not let this remark anger me, as may have been intended. I lowered my shawl as if I would make myself at home.

'You have very little area for entertainment, I see.'

'Linette, make the young lady comfortable at the foot of the bed,' he ordered his daughter in a gentle tone totally lacking in the mockery he used toward me and even toward Sister Magdalen.

'But Papa, you never let them sit down!' the girl cried, making me self-conscious.

Her frankness did not seem to disturb her father

who agreed in excellent humour, 'Exactly so, my love.' He pretended to cuff her unruly head of straight brown hair, then shifted his legs under the blanket, leaving a generous place for me, but I sat down carefully, not liking to crowd him. I was the intruder, after all.

'Now then,' he said, as Linette plumped up the harsh homespun cover of the pillow behind his dark head, 'you are going to persuade me that I can sell my daughter at whatever the current rate may be. That is to say, several thousand assignats higher than yesterday's offer.'

'Assignats are practically worthless these days,' I told him.

He glanced at me and then away, at Linette's head. 'An honest emissary as a change. Linette, we are living in strange times.'

I did not rise to the bait and he was apparently too curious, or possibly intrigued, by my unorthodox behaviour to wait for my proposal.

'Citizeness, why *did* you come to this hell if not to bargain for my daughter?'

'I came to see you, to see if your refusal was genuine. Then I would decide whether to take the principessa's offer or not.'

My frankness kept surprising him, it seemed.

'And have you decided?'

'No. I imagine your daughter knows your circumstances. May I speak frankly?'

He laughed. 'You have hardly been reticent so far. Yes, Linette knows.' The girl reached out her hand and he took it. In spite of the jauntiness he presented to the world, I saw that even the slight pressure of squeezing his daughter's fingers cost him some effort. 'If you please, speak frankly, Citizeness. You haven't given us your name yet.'

'Clare Dubeque. And I am not an actress with the Comédie Française.'

'Ah! That accusation bit deep, I see.' And the idea amused him.

'On the contrary,' I said. 'If I were employed as an actress, I should not have been forced to listen to the Principessa Visconti's offer.' He started to say something, perhaps to congratulate me again on my penchant for truth-telling, but I went on quickly. 'So far as I was concerned, and if I had accepted her offer, I saw no harm in escorting your daughter to Milano. Now, I must ask you: what will happen to your daughter when you die?'

'He won't! He won't ever!' Linette cried, her eyes snapping.

'Sweetheart, don't talk nonsense,' her father chided her gently. 'We have always been honest. No lies between us.'

I bit my lip and stared hard at the stripes in my skirt. I had seldom disliked myself so much. 'I won't apologise. It was a dreadful thing to say. But it must be faced. You must make some plan. Even more so if you dislike the principessa so much.' I started to get up.

He seemed to have had a change of heart and stopped me with a few words spoken in a voice that moved me so deeply I felt I would never forget them. 'Don't go. Please. We may need you.'

I took a deep breath. 'I won't try to force you to give her up. Nor will I attempt to persuade you. But if I can help in any way . . . ' I remembered something, and told the father and daughter directly. 'It may be of interest to you that I owe the principessa nothing, not even the very handsome fifty English pounds to be exchanged for French livres in Geneva. That was to have been earnest pay, an earnest of my becoming her employee.'

Marius Redon's eyes opened wide in reaction to the sum of fifty pounds.

'And you are so wealthy you can afford to delay in your acceptance?'

'If I am to eat and to sleep through the month's end, for a little over two weeks, I must spend no more than five sous a day. As to the next year – ' I shrugged. 'I have not yet discovered just how I will be employed in the shining new nineteenth century, but I must be capable of something.'

There was a little pause. No doubt Marius Redon was puzzled by my failure to accept the offer of fifty pounds. He must believe me, but his tone told me he wisely gave the matter a light touch. It was not his affair.

'Linette, we must put our minds to it. What can Citizeness Dubeque find to occupy herself until the new century?'

'She's different from the others. Not so pretty as some that came, but . . . well . . .'

Both Marius and I laughed. Marius said quickly, 'Citizeness Clare is not pretty because she is beautiful. There is a distinction, I am happy to say.' While Linette was considering this verdict, with which it was clear she did not agree, her father looked at me. I was certain he was about to begin some quite sensible conversation but then his cheerful expression faded. He glanced up at someone opening the drape behind me. 'Not so soon, my love! Not nearly so soon. We have settled nothing yet.'

I looked behind me apprehensively, but I had already guessed that Sister Magdalen was here to order me out. At the same time the great hall began to darken, and the roar of voices broke into distinct sounds of protest. Even as I stood, the nun reached over beyond Linette and snuffed a tallow candle.

By the single flickering lamp somewhere outside the cubicle, I saw Marius Redon's eyes studying me thoughtfully. I was about to leave with a brief

47

goodbye but was surprisingly touched when he put out his hand to me. I scarcely knew what to do with it, but the gesture seemed warm and friendly. I put my own fingers into his. He returned to the light, teasing tone he had used when we met.

'I daresay we have seen the last of you. You will not be brave enough to make your way through this labyrinth again.'

'Certainly not by the door I chose tonight.'

'But another way?'

I was not unmoved by his charm, but I managed to remind him, 'Is our business unfinished then?'

'Very much so.'

I laughed, promising to return, and he released my hand.

As I was leaving, I heard Sister Magdalen suggest to Linette that her bed was ready and she too must go. The girl began to protest and I could guess the painful scene that would follow. When I knew the Redons better, perhaps I might be able to help them without involving the principessa. But I doubted that I could persuade Linette to leave her father. There might not be much time left to them.

The thought was suddenly painful. I tried to banish it as I made my way with difficulty toward the front of the crowded hall. By this time, however, the inmates were settling down for the night with astonishing success. I could already hear any number of snores on different, not unmusical notes. I hurried down the steps and out upon the deserted street.

The city was silent and dark between little pockets of noise and gaiety across the bridge to the Right Bank and the area leading to the old Palais-Royal Arcades. My side of the river, across the bridge in the Latin Quarter, was so dark I was lucky to know my way almost by a sense of touch.

I walked rapidly, trying to ignore the dreadful

pools of darkness on the Cité before I crossed the bridge to my own quarter. In those dark pools there were sounds betraying the presence of night-creatures. I could even see the eyes, the whites of those eyes gleaming now and then as they caught a vagrant light from one of the river banks. I found it curious that none of these cut-throats made an effort to seize my reticule for the few coins it contained, or my shawl which would be worth something.

But as I finally reached my own narrow street, I did look back once, and understood why no one had touched me. My trouble was already following me in the form of that ferret-faced little man employed by the Principessa Visconti. The criminals of the Cité island did not interfere with what they supposed to be a fellow criminal's victim.

CHAPTER FOUR

MY dreams were somewhat incoherent that night and all I could remember was that Marius Redon was in them, and his daughter as well. The moment I awoke in the morning I thought of the pair of them, living out what remained of his life in that dreadful Hôtel Dieu where even the windows were sealed up with ancient piles of refuse and old furniture. There might be some arrangement he could make, or that the government could make, about removing him to a less crowded hospital in which he might prolong his life, or even recover.

There were moments during my visit when Marius Redon had shown such spirit and vivacity that I thought it would be a double tragedy for such a man to die. Surely one so young and so vital need not die! Fate was unjust.

I was astonished at the violence of my own emotions about this matter. I had been in the company of Marius Redon and his daughter scarcely an hour, yet here I was, suddenly waving my fist at fate over these strangers. Marius Redon had won me over exactly as Thérèse Tallien and Sylvie had prophesied. I was like Sister Magdalen, captive despite myself.

The Auvergnat water-seller came by calling out his wares as I finished dressing, and I rushed to my narrow balcony and sent down a large decanter on the strong hemp that served me in such matters. Even as I did so, adding my smallest coins to pay

51

for the drinking and washing water, I found myself wondering if the water given to the hospital patients was also reasonably pure, or were they given the tainted water from the Seine?

There were so many things I did not know about my own native city. What did the Redons eat? Was the food decent and healthful? At the time of my parents' imprisonment they were permitted to pay for the most delicious food to be delivered from one of our best cafés. There was little difference between the Conciergerie and the Hôtel Dieu, as far as I could see.

I went down to have my breakfast at a small café in the Place Michel, and to think. It was much cheaper to dine on my bread and chocolate prepared by the Rights of Man Café, formerly The King's Arms, than to have it brought to my room. And there was Gervase, the waiter-owner, who had given me excellent advice for years, chief of which was that no lady should be seen in a café. That cold, sunny December morning, as I settled myself just within the door with a view of the busy square outside, I broached a subject that had never been more pertinent.

'Gervase, it comes to this. I must work.'

'Ma petite, marry me. It is easier than finding employment for a female born into your class.' He set down the small round loaf of new-baked bread and the little jug of foaming chocolate.

I sniffed the chocolate while murmuring my whole-hearted appreciation. It smelled heavenly.

'If I marry you, Gervase, it will be for your chocolate.'

He beamed. The big, broad-faced taverner had been a violent section leader during the early days of the Terror, but the years had mellowed him. He was now a passionate supporter of the more moderate First Consul Bonaparte.

'Ma petite Clare, is this an acceptance? The banns shall be posted at once.'

'What? A religious ceremony? Gervase, you would be drummed out of Paris. Not even General Bonaparte can bring that about.' I poured and began to drink the chocolate from one of the cracked cups whose history had once troubled me. I knew Gervase had discovered them during one of the street riots of the September Massacres. But we all lived in a brutal world, and had accommodated ourselves to that world, including the cups that had doubtless belonged to one of the victims.

And now, would I let Marius Redon die and his daughter be reared in some frightful place like the Hôtel Dieu, and do nothing?

'I am quite in earnest, my friend. I must earn money in order to live. Otherwise,' I shrugged, 'there will be no New Century for me.' I tore off pieces of the fresh bread. It was still dark and coarse, but far superior to that we had eaten a few years ago.

Gervase insisted that marriage to him was the answer, but he said it jokingly. He had been married long ago to a powerful, loud-voiced woman who ran his life as she ran his café, and her death of a fever several years ago had not plunged him into very protracted mourning.

'I must think on the business of a post for you,' he said finally, as other patrons sauntered in to find their own table. 'But it may be that you would do better to accept the old woman's offer.' Someone at a bench against the far wall called to him and he left me.

He also left me speechless, chilled with apprehension. So the Principessa Visconti's long fingers had reached out and pinched at my old friend, Gervase! I had not thought it possible. I sat there absently breaking up bits of bread and drinking my chocolate but I was asking myself why, if the princess was in earnest about caring for her late husband's great-granddaughter, and about the wickedness of the child's uncle, she stooped to so much bribery to achieve her ends. Why did Marius Redon mistrust her? Of course, it might be simply that Marius did not want to lose his daughter's company so long as he maintained his dogged hold on life.

How much had the principessa offered Gervase, one of the few people I had trusted? But then, I could not really trust anyone. Life had taught me that.

Gervase threaded his way back to my table from a soldier and a thinly clad young woman in the *merveilleuse* style who were sitting close on a settee against the far wall. I wondered if I would be permitted to bring food to Linette Redon and her father in the hospital. I must have appeared absorbed in my thoughts, because Gervase was uneasy. He spoke more rapidly than was his custom.

'You are concerned over something, ma belle? Tell old Gervase. You must trust old—' He broke off. He must have realised that he had reminded me that I could *not* trust him.

I looked up at his wide, bland face that was all innocence and I was sure he was thoroughly prepared to lie.

'Gervase, what did the princess' agents pay you?'

'Pay? Me? My dear Clare, you know me better. I am not a man to take a bribe. Gervase Martin is no man's pawn!'

'Then why did you suggest that I accept the old woman's offer?'

His heavy shoulders stiffened. He began a feeble lie, stumbling for an explanation. Failing, he admitted sheepishly, 'It is so. A little rat of a fellow came by as I was at the shutters this morning. Offered me a handful of assignats.'

'They are worthless.'

'So I told him. What did he take me for? Made him give me the livres that the new government is issuing. Twenty livres.' He studied my face, saw that I had not thawed. I was furious at this pointless hounding. That he had begun to earn his twenty livres, I liked even less. His big hands fluttered all around me as he said earnestly, 'You would do well to accept the offer. Why do you refuse? Think of the advantages, ma petite. The estate the child would inherit. Fantastic, they say. And as her companion who defended her nobly, you would no doubt be paid a handsome sum afterward.'

I cut into his rambling. 'After what?' I had intended merely to stop this flow of unwanted rhetoric. It was after I asked the question that a horrid suspicion came to me and I repeated very quietly, 'After what, Gervase?'

'But after the child's delivery, of course. What else could I have meant? What else would they tell me, a stranger to them? I am not in their confidence. Not yet, at all events. Will you have more chocolate? Let me bring you another pot.'

It was useless to waste time and emotion on Gervase. I recovered enough not to reveal how deeply concerned I was.

'Gervase, could you sell me another of the small loaves and another pot of chocolate, and lend me a basket and napkin? One of those nice fringed ones?'

Obviously relieved that I had changed the subject, he fussed around eagerly, rubbing a filthy, wet towel over my table, polishing the aged wooden surface, all around the stain left by the chocolate jug.

'Nothing easier, as to the chocolate. But there was the devil's own queue outside the baker's shop. I was lucky to get my loaves. However,' he slapped the cloth hard upon the table, splashing me, 'for my favourite female, it shall be done. You must have one of my remaining loaves. Let one of my other patrons complain. What is that to me? You will take this basket for a picnic in the Luxembourg Gardens, perhaps.' Then a shocking thought occurred to him. 'You go with a man. Who is my rival? Present him to me. I will snap him in two. So!' He demonstrated so fiercely that I laughed as he went off to arrange the basket.

When he returned there were several new patrons waiting for him, one of whom I was very probably depriving of his breakfast. I didn't want to be present at the uproar which would follow, so I took the basket and paid for its contents, promising to bring the basket back, as well as the jug and the napkin. I turned down my own little street so that Gervase would not guess my destination. But I had to hurry. Although the jug was sealed, its contents might cool before I reached the hospital.

In spite of the sunlight it was a winter world, with a brisk wind and a cold that seeped into the bones. The trees were stark and dead, but there was a renewed spirit about the city, all the same: improvements everywhere, especially the quais along the river, and the look of optimistic expectation on the faces of the citizens. They inspired me to a similar optimism.

A sharp gust off the river slapped me in the face and caught the deep brim of my bonnet so that I nearly lost my balance. I clutched my bonnet brim with my free hand while trying not to upset the basket in the crook of my right arm. My clumsiness made oncoming pedestrians laugh, and lifted me to an unaccustomed mood of elation. I walked on under the blue December sky, oddly excited as I passed the slums around Notre Dame and approached the great, grey Hôtel Dieu.

There was far less activity around the front of

the hospital this morning. Perhaps I was too early to get in. Just before I stepped up to challenge what dragon doorkeepers there might be, I looked back carefully over the street activity but could not make out anyone who resembled last night's indefatigable, ferret-faced little man. I should have been relieved, but the truth is, my inability to spot him only made me wonder where he might be hidden. A street sweeper moved along the gutter wielding his long, curved broomstraws. He looked extraordinarily like the principessa's spy until I caught sight of his face. He was much too old.

The doorkeeper appeared to be a jolly friar, but jolly or not, he refused me admission. I tried persuasion, showed him by basket, and found that was a mistake. Still smiling, he attempted to remove the basket from my arm, thanking me all the while. We had begun a pulling match, and I was becoming afraid poor Gervase would never see his basket again, when the imposing figure of Sister Magdalen appeared and lent her authority to my side of the dispute.

'Mademoiselle is expected. Follow me, if you please.'

I obeyed hurriedly, but I could see that I had arrived before other visitors. The patients who could afford meals sent in were eating or being fed from trays by waiters from the nearby cafés. Other patients made do with the porridge and wine furnished by the State. In spite of the limitations of diet, it seemed evident to me that this was one of the bright moments of the patients' day. But I thought the many sealed-up windows must be more than a little depressing. The night candles had all been snuffed so that the complex series of partitioned alcoves and cubicles was completely dependent upon the few uncluttered windows for illumination.

'How are the Redons this morning?' I asked Sister Magdalen.

'The basket is for them?'

She did not appear to disapprove. Except in the presence of Marius Redon, she kept a tight rein upon emotions of any sort.

'Yes, if you permit it, Sister. I was not certain what foods the patients received. I did not mean to intrude upon the work of the hospital.'

'You do not intrude. I believe your visit was of definite aid to the patient. As for his daughter, I cannot be certain.'

This was an unexpected blow. 'Oh, no!' I protested anxiously. 'Is Linette ill?'

'Not ill, but I suspect she is a trifle jealous. For some time now every visitor has been disliked by her father. But suddenly you appeared and before her eyes Linette saw an improvement in her father. A new hold upon life. I hope, Mademoiselle – ' She turned and looked at me directly. 'I hope you are not about to betray them. I am certain they have enemies. I would not like to think you were actually one of those enemies.'

'I swear to you, Sister, by – by the salvation of my mother, the most solemn oath I can think of – that I wish to be their friend. I will not knowingly betray them.' The words rushed out in my desire for her to believe me, to know I wanted to be their friend.

She stared at me before we started up to the floor above. 'I accept your word, Mademoiselle,' she said simply, and we walked up together. There was a small window halfway up the steps and this unsatisfactory light was our sole illumination. The lower floor smelled vile from bodies and sickness. I wondered how often, if ever, it was cleaned. On the upper floor things were a trifle better, though the illumination was as depressing as it might have been in a dreary November twilight. Some of the cots and the bedclothes were piled against temporary partitions or against the chill hospital walls.

I saw several soldiers and two officers sprinkled among the male patients, and I hurried my steps to match Sister Magdalen's almost masculine stride.

'Sister, why are the soldiers here?'

She paid little attention except to remark, 'General Bonaparte insists there must be improved treatment for the wounded. The soldiers who are dropped here with the rest of our patients are to be removed to hospitals set up for the military. Experiments will be performed on them to save limbs which would otherwise be sawed off. There have been some surprising cures already, and we certainly need the space.'

'And – and Marius Redon? Was he not one of General Bonaparte's captains?'

'Quite true, but I doubt it will be worth removing him. However, the General is most attentive. He has given orders for every comfort that is possible. The Captain does have privacy, food, linens. A laundress comes daily for his linens by order of the general. It is a matter of some importance to a man like the Captain.'

'I'm sure that it is.' But I was beginning to feel a little foolish about Gervase's basket. Still, I could always give the food to other patients.

'Is there no hope then for Captain Redon?' I ventured, after failing in my resolve to keep silent about the man.

'Hope?' She glanced across the room to a far alcove where I saw a carved wooden crucifix in a tiny niche above the pillow of a bedridden patient. She did not answer me directly.

Even as I waited for her answer, I found my tension far in excess of any right I had to be concerned in this man's life or death. Had a simple handclasp accomplished so much? Or was I reacting so violently because I believed I had lost Paul Vallier's love and was receptive to the practised charm of the first handsome stranger I met?

Sister Magdalen glanced at me. Her fine, large eyes looked suddenly naked to me. She did care very much, though her voice remained noncommittal.

'He is in my prayers, Mademoiselle. We can do no more.'

It was no answer to a woman like me, or at best, only half an answer. I had grown up through a world in revolution. My parents had been staunch revolutionary idealists whose faith lay in mankind, not in religious panaceas. I could not but share their beliefs. My own instinct was to rely upon practical medication plus prayer. That way, one could be doubly armed.

'Ah!' she said, as we turned a corner and arrived before that wretched cubicle with its faded crimson drape. 'We arrive.' In front of the curtain she called out, 'Monsieur Marius, a visitor.'

The voices of Marius and his daughter in the midst of some sort of game ceased abruptly. Linette whispered something. Marius said quite audibly, 'Good God! I hope not!'

A fine beginning. I hoisted the basket and almost turned away. Sister Magdalen caught the sleeve of my pelisse. This time she very nearly smiled.

'Monsieur Marius? Mademoiselle Dubeque is here.'

There was a sound of rustling beyond the drape. To my intense relief and some amusement, I heard someone, Linette probably, smoothing her father's bed. There was a silence, then Linette's command, 'Now!'

We stepped inside to find Marius Redon sitting up in bed with a deck of playing cards in front of him. The scene was cosy and charming, even to the clean white shirt he wore, with the cuff frills carefully ironed, just as the Sister had told me. The snowy white of the shirt did nothing for the sallowness of his skin, but it was exceedingly romantic by contrast with his eyes and hair. He held out his hand to take mine, and when I extended my free hand, I thought he would put my fingers to his lips in the gallant fashion of the Old Regime. He seemed about to do so, but he held my fingers briefly, then let them go.

This welcome was delightfully affecting, but I was dismayed to glimpse a tray of dishes that had been set back on a little cabinet. I had a strong inclination to hide the basket behind me, but Linette had already seen it. Before she could say anything, I began to slide the basket handles down over my wrist.

'I must appear quite absurd, but I had such an excellent breakfast, I thought a duplicate would not go amiss. No matter. I am too late.'

Marius Redon's warm, slow smile that did not quite reach his eyes, was reward enough.

'Linette and I thank you from our hearts, Citizeness.'

Linette had peered into the basket and under the napkin. She sniffed curiously.

'Oh, Papa, it's chocolate. You hate chocolate.'

Marius sighed at this undiplomatic truth, then caught my eye and we both laughed. I was about to turn the basket over to Sister Magdalen when Linette hinted strongly, 'But I don't hate chocolate. We didn't have any for breakfast. We had nasty coffee.'

Coffee was luxury indeed. The general did look out for his men.

After a little discussion, Sister Magdalen suggested that Linette drink the chocolate and Marius eat some of the bread before it became stale in another hour or two. When she had gone, Marius broke off bits of bread and began to eat. I seated myself in my now familiar place on the end of his bed, avoiding his crossed legs under the blanket. We were all silent for a few minutes, companionably silent.

Marius broke the silence unexpectedly. 'Citizeness Clare, Linette is very much in need of a little fresh air. What is your opinion of fresh air?'

For a few seconds I didn't understand his purpose in the question. He flexed his fingers and moved his arms in such a way as to give me a hint, and I suggested casually, 'I think it can be most useful. Would you trust me with your daughter for an hour or two?'

He brightened. 'Just so.' He glanced furtively at the drape where Sister Magdalen had disappeared. 'I feel infinitely better today and I don't want my good dragons to breathe fire upon my plans.'

'Father!' Linette demanded suspiciously. 'What are you about?'

Her father hesitated, looking guilty, and I was certain he intended to get out of bed, to stand or perhaps even walk. He was afraid to have Linette or Sister Magdalen see him; for their love and affection would prevent his accomplishing any physical exertions. I knew what he intended was dangerous, but that the alternatives were not very encouraging; so, with some qualms, I silently agreed to co-operate in his plans, hoping that he might profit by forcing the strength back into his limbs. I thought of it as precisely that: a forcing of health, a monumental fight against death. And my admiration for Marius Redon rose by each moment I was in his company.

'Wouldn't you like to walk to the Luxembourg Gardens?' I suggested to Linette. 'Some fresh air will put roses in your cheeks.'

'I had rather see them in Papa's face.'

Before either Marius or I could make the mistake of laughing at her plaintive remark, he said with a kind of playful seriousness, 'But gentlemen are not expected to have roses in their cheeks. Now, my linnet, my very special Linette, you will make my day much happier if you go with Citizeness Clare.' He looked at me. 'Do you object very much to my calling you Clare?'

'It is exceedingly improper,' Linette put in on a prim, adult note.

Marius glanced at me but the humour I read was masked for his daughter's benefit.

'Most improper, except among old friends. Let us pretend the Citizeness is an old friend.'

'Very old,' I added.

'Well . . . ' But it was perfectly obvious her father had won her over.

I suggested that she wear a heavy cloak. 'There was a strong wind over the river. It nearly took my bonnet with it. I thought for a minute that I should find myself floating over the city like a balloonist.'

With her father's help she was putting her thin, brittle young arms into the sleeves of her brown pelisse, but she giggled at my picture of a lady balloonist floating above the chimney pots of Paris. When she was ready we had another small problem. She did not want to leave her father. Rather daringly, I slapped the blanket over Marius Redon's legs and said briskly, 'I shall be speaking with Sister Magdalen, Linette . . .Citizeness Linette.' To her father I was even more brisk. 'Two hours. Be discreet, Captain.'

'Discretion in all things,' he promised me, and this time his eyes were definitely smiling.

I waited outside the draped cubicle, deliberately too far away to hear their voices. Linette came out a minute or two later. She looked much too tense and white. I reached out for her hand in its mended

63

glove, but she drew it away and tucked it between the buttons of her pelisse. The gesture had not been a deliberate affront, but a reminder that I must not assume too many liberties. We were not such good friends as all that!

I tried a cheerful line, which was a mistake.

'In two hours we shall be returning and you will feel infinitely better.'

'Me! How can that matter?' She took a deep breath. Her face looked stiff and cold as she added with vehemence, 'If Marius gets sick while I am away from him, I'll never, never forgive you! Don't you see? If he must die, he mustn't die by himself. I must be there.'

I shocked myself by the loudness of my reply. 'He will not die. He is going to live and get well!'

She looked at me wide-eyed, shocked, I think, by my forcefulness. The sudden flicker of hope I read there disturbed me; I had promised a great deal.

In a subdued manner she said, 'Last night I went out alone, a nasty little man tried to take me prisoner. I bit his hand. If he tries again, will you bite him?'

This was a new danger I hadn't counted on, but I was completely serious when I promised, 'I shall bite just as hard as you did, or harder. Because I am older than you and my bite would be tougher than yours.'

This time she giggled in earnest.

CHAPTER FIVE

ALTHOUGH I looked around the street and off toward the far Right Bank as we left the hospital, I saw no suspicious signs, but the street and the area around the hospital were crowded. We made our way to the bridge, glancing at the imposing façade of Notre Dame which had stood empty and desecrated for so long. It was good to see the flicker of candles within as the great portals opened for an unobtrusive service.

We crossed the Pont-Double to the Latin Quarter and walked up toward the Gardens. By the time I had convinced myself no one cared in the least about us, I noticed that Linette was now greatly interested in everyone who passed us. We came upon the gates suddenly, out of a narrow, winding street, and went in after a stout female accompanied by a girl somewhat younger than Linette. The woman wore what once had been a pointed Phrygian bonnet, a symbol of the bloodthirsty market women during the Terror, but the blood colour had faded to pink and there was a mended place on the side of the bonnet where, until recently, the tricolour rosette had been sewn.

The woman turned and grinned at Linette and me, flashing a set of gums with a scarcity of teeth. I nodded and smiled a greeting in return but was surprised and would have been pleased at Linette's hand sneaking quietly into my own, except that I suspected she was frightened by the woman, and that should not be. The woman and the girl moved south into the wintry heart of the gardens, while Linette exclaimed breathlessly, 'Tell me about the place. What a very large, cold place it looks!'

The Luxembourg Palace at the near end of the gardens had been the prison which briefly held my father's friend from the Cordeliers Club, Camille Desmoulins, and I was a bit snappish about it.

'It houses some government offices now. I believe the First Consul was here until recently. Very gloomy. Linette, that woman we met at the gate was quite harmless, you know. She is undoubtedly hired to care for the child.'

'What? But Clare, she looked such a lady! Well, not a lady, perhaps, but one of the *merveilleuses*. All those bright yellow curls. I thought they might be false. And I've seen her before.'

I had a sudden stabbing notion that we were talking about my almost-sister, Sylvie Vallier. I swung around. And there she was, Sylvie! All tinkling gold and sounding brass.

'Clare, chérie, at last! Do you know how long I have been strolling about these dreary walks, waiting for you?' She would have embraced me but Linette was in her way. The girl stared at Sylvie and then at me and slowly withdrew her hand from mine.

'You are friends?' She sounded incredulous and horrified. I tried to recover Linette's confidence, but in vain. She had taken a violent and fearful dislike to Sylvie.

I said more calmly than I felt, 'I did not intend to meet Citizeness Vallier here or elsewhere. I don't in the least understand you, Sylvie. How did you discover I was to be in the Gardens? I did not decide to come here until an hour ago.'

Sylvie fluttered her silk shawl in the breeze, winding it around her sinuous form. She was all hurt surprise, but she fooled neither of us. The difference was that I became distinguished, but Linette was clearly terrified.

'You really do know her!' Linette murmured with a disbelief that baffled me.

'You haven't answered me,' I reminded Sylvie.

She was very frank about it, 'I asked your friend Gervase. He told me you intended to picnic here.'

So my lie to Gervase had caught me up! I was breathless for a moment and Linette stared at me, guessing the truth of Sylvie's claim even before I made a lame but indignant excuse. 'I had entirely forgotten. When I told Gervase that, it was to keep him from discovering where I—What do you want of me, Sylvie?'

'Chérie, I know quite well how important your love is to you. I have been trying to make it easier. Now, you go about it very clearly. The path of an obliging friend and all of that.'

How could she possibly know about Marius Redon? I had only met him last night. Could she read my mind? My heart?

After a stunned few seconds I said coolly, 'Don't be ridiculous. I scarcely know—'

And she cut me off, perplexed for the first time.

'But Clare, it is true one does not know a man until one lives with him, but surely, after all these years, you can be said to know our Paul.'

I must have turned crimson. I had entirely forgotten that, in the world of our little group, I was still betrothed to Paul Vallier!

'Sylvie, I don't wish to seem rude, but you are interrupting us. The young lady and I are studying the history of this place.' I prayed she would not recognise Linette Redon, but suspected Sylvie's friends had informed her of every facet in their conspiracy. If, of course, it was a conspiracy. I had no real proof that Marius Redon's suspicions were based on fact. For all I knew, the Principessa

67

Visconti might be speaking the truth. She wanted Linette Redon safely restored to the fortune and estate that were hers by law and by the Visconti will. It was natural that Marius should want to keep his daughter by him as long as he could, and in order to keep her, he would imagine the worst of those who wanted to take her from him.

'Clare, think! With two hundred pounds – well, whatever that is, it is more than you have seen in years – you could live as you should. A lady, worthy of your future husband. And it is all for the best interests of the child. She will be one of the greatest heiresses in Europe.'

'You may as well forget the notion. Her father does not trust the princess. Nor do I if it comes to that.'

Sylvie fingered the fringe of her shawl. 'You must be mad!'

'No, only thinking seriously. Something Gervase said to me this morning makes me wonder what is really intended by these friends of yours.'

Her gasp sounded genuine. 'What did he say? Tell me!' She had the audacity to take my shoulders in an attempt to shake me.

'*Take your hands from me!*'

Surprised and a little frightened, I think, she backed off and I turned around, saying in a changed voice, 'I'll take you home now.' But Linette Redon was gone.

Had she run away when she found she couldn't trust me? Or worse, had Sylvie kept me talking while the princess' evil little spy seized Linette? I was terrified, and murderously angry.

'Are you responsible? Did your friends take her?' I raised one hand and she ducked instinctively.

'No, no, Clare. I swear it! I was to come and persuade you. Nothing else. She must have run off by herself. Clare, where are you going? Clare!'

I swung around, looking everywhere. Linette was not in sight. To have disappeared this quickly she must have left the garden by the near gates. I started to run. Outside the gates, I thought I saw her far ahead, toward the river. I don't believe I stopped rushing over those cobblestones until I reached the Seine itself.

I was forced to pause at the junction of several alleys in front of Notre Dame, frantic at the delay which kept me from making certain Linette had reached the hospital in safety. So I stood uncomfortably shoved among a score of other Parisians while a wooden tumbrel, emptied of cabbages, was raised from its side and set on its rickety wheels again. A crowd was gathering to rescue and steal the cabbages while the ancient mare stood calmly nuzzling the pastry tray carried by a gaping baker's boy.

After an eternity of ten minutes or so, I was able to break through and make my way to the Hôtel Dieu. I had thought nothing worse could happen after losing Linette Redon, but the greatest blow was yet to come.

No guard was at the big doors. This puzzled me but I supposed it was because I had arrived at the visitors' hour. I had not yet reached the staircase when Sister Magdalen rushed toward me, seizing my hand and tumbling the questions out. 'How did it happen? How did they take her without your knowledge? Did you see?'

'Sister! I knew nothing. I was stopped by the sister of the man to whom I was – am betrothed. I quarrelled with her because she seemed to have been following us. When I looked around, Linette was gone. Tell me! What is it? Does Citizen Marius know? He must not! It would be so very bad for—'

She raised her hands to stop me. 'Too late!'

'What! But he mustn't know! Hasn't she returned?'

'Worse. You see, Monsieur Marius had got up and dressed, and was walking about most unwisely, against my advice. But he did seem to be gaining strength. Then, a little thin-faced man came a few minutes ago. He asked Monsieur Marius to sign a document surrendering his daughter to the guardianship of her great-grandmother. Monsieur Marius very properly refused and the little man made some threat. I could not hear it. But I am in terror for Monsieur. He rushed off, telling me he must recover his child. "I know the old harridan in the Rue St Honoré has her", he said, and I lost him among all those visitors below stairs.'

'Good God! He will kill himself! But I know the place. *Rue St Honoré.*' I turned to go but Sister Magdalen's voice, sharp with worry, called after me, 'I think I may have given him some aid. Monsieur Marius is well liked among his army comrades. Three of them came from General Bonaparte's offices only minutes after he left, so I sent them after him.'

'Pray they catch him! Because I will certainly make them surrender the child,' I promised her, and started away through a crowd of playing children. I was not boasting with that promise. If necessary, I was determined to go to the aides of the First Consul, General Bonaparte himself, and bring force into play against them all, including Paul's meddling sister. If the princess and her little band of conspirators planned to snatch Linette out of Paris, a word from the First Consul's office to the Prefect of the Seine could close every one of the Barriers of Paris. I would not hesitate to jog that awesome power.

There was no possibility of hiring a carriage, and it would never get through the midday traffic anyway. I hurried across the Cité to the Pont au Change and crossed it, looking like a hoyden with my bonnet blown off my head and suspended by its cherry-coloured ribbons. I never crossed this bridge if I could avoid it. It was the route of the tumbrel whose destination had been the two uprights in the Place de la Révolution called 'The National Razor.' Even now, long afterward, the route was painful for me, but I was in a great hurry.

On the Right Bank I was slowed by the stalls of old clothing, fresh vegetables, used furnishings and bric-a-brac that extended from the seamed and aged buildings to the middle of the serpentine streets. I took a moment to breathe deeply and to massage the stitch in my side. Then, under the shocked stare of an elderly female at a carriage window, and the amused gaze of a tall, mustachioed grenadier, I made my way between two stalls, past a corner café and into the Rue St Honoré.

Here I thought I caught sight of the three soldiers Sister Magdalen had mentioned, but they turned in toward the Place du Carrousel where the Consular Guard Grenadiers had just completed their midday review. The crowd that usually witnessed this colourful sight was breaking up now to cause still greater confusion in this busy sector of the city.

Disappointed at my mistake about the soldiers I had counted on to help their captain, I wondered if I would have to seek out the aid of the General's office after all. Finally, I came into sight of the townhouse in which Sylvie Vallier lodged, and where I assumed the princess was staying. I had not yet reached the building when a surge of excitement broke from within and poured out onto the crowded street.

I saw the uniforms first. These must be the men of Marius Redon's company. But had they arrived too late? They were laughing, making a great commotion, pushing and cuffing each other. Marius suddenly appeared among them, holding Linette by the hand. She was looking up at him with admiration, and some anxiety too. But whatever exertions must have taken place in that house had by no means defeated him. He looked dreadfully tired, with dark smudges under his eyes, but there was about him the air of a captain in the army that had swept in triumph over half of Europe. The confidence was there and the quiet determination. I saw for the first time that he was a man of middle height, trim but not, thank heaven, gaunt. As he and his comrades approached, I realised that he had spent nearly all his angry, burning energy, but he was obviously determined to walk back to the hospital.

Now they came abreast of me. The soldiers glanced at me with curiosity, but I was hoping only for a chance to offer a few words of explanation to Marius and his daughter. As Linette caught sight of me, she drew closer to her father. It was he who shocked me. He looked at me with sombre eyes and a little smile so full of contempt that I hope I may never again see or feel such disillusionment directed to me. I could not say a word in my defence. They had all passed me before I recovered. I felt wounded at his loss of faith in me, but I understood.

After debating with myself over the best course of action, I did not follow Marius. I went on to that town house acquired by Sylvie through some machinations of the former Director of the government, Citizen Barras. He did a lively trade in the properties of aristocratic émigrés. I felt such fury at the goings-on of the principessa and her coterie that I decided to play the spy in earnest, and to give any information I gleaned to Marius Redon. Whether he would believe me, or use the information, was up to him.

By the time I reached Sylvie's house the commotion was over, but several women from a market nearby were still arguing the exciting events they had witnessed.

'I came to deliver the day's fish,' said one. 'Good pay, you know. None of those paper assignats. And here on that landing was the old woman shrieking like a – like a – '

'Fishwife?' suggested another woman slyly. The fishwife made a fist as if to strike her friend but then threw back her tousled head and laughed. 'That may be. But those soldier-boys took the tongue-lashing in good humour. Ah! Our soldier-boys were that handsome, you'd not believe! And the one with the child, he took her with him – his daughter, they say – and away they all clattered, down the stairs to the street. The Old One screamed she was the grandmother and the child was hers. But you could see the child feared her and adored the young soldier.'

'As good a show as the Theâtre Feydau,' said one of the women as they passed me and the little group broke up in the street.

I went up the stairs. The door to the foyer of Sylvie's apartment was still ajar, but I heard no shouting within, just a murmur of voices. The principessa's group was evidently considering its next step. The foyer door creaked as I grasped the latch, pushing the door open, and everyone in the salon jumped nervously, looking toward me. The sunlight of mid-afternoon provided considerable light through the long windows but left the foyer in shadow and I don't think they identified me for a few seconds.

'Good day to you, one and all,' I said brightly. I found my voice quite unrecognisable to my own ears, but they noticed nothing amiss. 'Were you successful?'

After a few seconds' frozen silence, Sylvie and the princess spoke together.

'How good to see you in such spirits, chérie!'

'Ah! Dear Paul's lovely mademoiselle! Do come in. Sylvie, child, see to your guest.'

Sylvie came fluttering to me before her maid could do so. 'The door was ajar,' I explained. 'I rapped, but I am afraid no one heard me.' I was amazed at my own lies but seeing that I had succeeded thus far, I continued, 'I came to apologise. I was rude to you in the Gardens today, Sylvie.'

'No, no. It was most understandable. What we planned hadn't been explained to you. As a matter of fact, Ridetti hadn't told me he intended to take the girl. But come, sit with us. We are in such trouble. You would scarcely credit it, after all our good intentions, our earnest attempts to bring that tiresome child to her inheritance.'

I am very much afraid I shivered as the principessa touched my arm, indicating that I should remain by her. Someone brought up a stiff, faded, brocade-covered chair and although I had never feared to sit by anyone else in the world, I had to force myself to take the chair, and to recall that with every word and every expression I must lie to this sharp-eyed old woman. I saw a hand removed from my chair and knew that the little man with the ferret-face was behind me. At least, I thought with a relief I dared not show, he had not succeeded in his attempt to steal Linette from her father; 'for her own good' as they were always careful to explain.

The principessa was sympathetic. 'You trembled, Mademoiselle. Are you chilled?'

'I'm afraid I stood near the Tuileries gates too long, watching the review of the Consular Guards. I had intended to come over here directly, but I was caught in the crowd. You see, Captain Redon wouldn't see me at the hospital. The Sister in charge said he refused. I think I must have realised then how stupid I had been to believe him. Such bad manners! So I came over to – to congratulate you. I think it is far the best thing for your grand-daughter.'

'My great-granddaughter, my dear.' She patted my hands. I firmly withstood the temptation to jerk them away. 'And so you agree to take the child? We can still throw her Uncle Bernardo off the scent.'

'But would it not be safer if you yourself were to escort Mademoiselle Linette?' I suggested, hoping to trap her.

'That seems to have failed us, as you see. Then, too, there is the small problem of Linette's dislike for me.'

'But if I should bring her to Milano safely, how will you persuade her to accept you?'

'Leave that to me, my child.'

It was said so flatly I almost shuddered.

'Now our whole scheme has gone for nothing,' Sylvie put in with breathless anger at the injustice of it all. Obviously, there was a profit in it for her. I pretended not to understand and then, in spite of the principessa's angry little gesture to keep silence, she babbled on, 'The rogue came and took her back. Seized the child almost out of her great-grandmama's arms. Of course, he had a troop of soldiers with him or he would never have succeeded.'

'I thought he was a dying man!' I exclaimed, unable to stifle the hope that they would prove me wrong.

'Possibly. He looked like death. But he did not act like it. If one did not know better, one would suspect his condition was not so serious. But my dear, it will now be more important than ever for you to retain the friendship of the fellow and our child, since it is clear he will not deal with us.'

I wondered how they thought Linette would react when she reached Milano with me, and found herself again in the principessa's hands. They must know she would hate them more than ever after today's frightening and absurd seizure. I wondered if I should mention this, and then realised that, like the principessa, I should express only the half-truth that seemed self-evident.

'If the child will not accept you now, how can you imagine she will accept you in Milano? You say it is your concern, but I think you have not considered the difficulties.'

The principessa nodded graciously. 'That is precisely how you will earn, if I may say so, your generous payment. You will have the long journey in which to persuade . . .'

'He will never let me take her. He will hate me.'

'Nonsense. You will have her by one means or another. You are to seek her out. Persuade her you were entirely innocent of the affair today. Condemn Ridetti, here.' She gestured toward the little man who looked at me with no expression in those marble eyes. 'Say that my love for her was so great I even accepted the plan of this dreadful man. You may say I will have him punished, and that I myself will place her and her fortune in the hands of anyone she chooses. Her father, of course, will be her choice. But all this, you must say, will come about once she has reached her estates.'

'And if he dies—'

'My dear naïve child! Of course, he will be dead by the time you and Linette arrive in Italy. That I can almost guarantee. But meantime, you will have acquired her confidence. You understand?'

I understood all too horribly. The pretence of danger from the mysterious Uncle Bernardo was gone. I had been initiated into the little coterie of conspirators. I felt my smile was frozen upon my lips in a hideous kind of grin.

'So it is all very simple, after all,' I said.

Sylvie was delighted. She clapped her hands. 'You are with us. Paul will be so happy you could oblige his friend. He wants so much to see you. You can meet in the Swiss cantons. I predict you will be married almost with the opening of our glorious new century.'

Over the body of the dead Marius Redon. If he did not obligingly die of natural causes within the next few days, it was clear to me that he would be assisted to his death by the order of my employer, the Principessa Visconti.

And what if he would not believe me? What if he persisted in going his way alone, trying to protect his daughter without the means to do so? He must believe me. His life and very possibly his daughter's life depended upon it!

CHAPTER SIX

BEFORE I left Sylvie's lodgings, I was asked if I thought I could persuade Linette to make the Alpine journey to her estates in Italy. I had no notion of how to reply to this, as there was a strong possibility that Marius Redon would not even read a note I wrote to him. I was certain he would not see me. So my hope of helping him and Linette with my spying activities was fairly dim. But I had to try. I had not forgotten that upon my first visit to the house in the Rue St Honoré mention had been made of an attempt to poison Linette. The princess could hardly be responsible for this if she were trying to remove Linette to Italy. That left the other and unknown enemy, Uncle Bernardo, about whom I knew nothing. Perhaps, in spite of all my suspicions, the princess had told me the truth about that enemy. They were undoubtedly rivals in some sense.

Upon my getting up to leave, I was offered but refused a glass of wine. 'Or ratafia, if you choose,' said the principessa, wrinkling her bony nose as her opinion of that palliative.

'Does Paul know of Your Highness' plans?' I asked, genuinely curious to discover if my betrothed had sunk so low. He was frank to an embarrassing degree, and the thought of his being part of this evil plan deeply troubled me. It would show that with his betrayal of his native land – as I thought of it – he had sunk morally to an abysmal degree.

'But certainly,' Sylvie insisted. 'He knows we are trying to bring the child to her rightful fortune.'

So Paul did not know of the slimy schemes behind that unselfish talk of Linette's fortune! I was much relieved.

'I will do whatever I can to win Captain Redon's trust again,' I promised them, and they could not know how honest that statement was.

'Excellent.' I was already on the stairs when the Principessa Visconti called after me. 'You should set out with Linette on Christmas morning. This will suit my own plans to perfection. The first payment should arrive at your lodgings this evening.'

I went away from that house and those people, those criminals whose plot against Marius Redon might only foreshadow something else even more ghastly. Of one thing I could never be sure, whether the little man named Ridetti was following me. I wanted to act correctly, as they pictured me, the dupe in all their plans; so I must do nothing that they would regard as unnatural. Oddly enough, my own plans meshed in almost every respect with their scheme.

I crossed through the old Feuillants Conventual property, now an endless tangle of huts, shacks, hovels and alleys crowding upon the desolate Tuileries Palace, and made my way to my own Latin Quarter without catching sight of anyone who might be spying on me. The afternoon light to the west of the city had all the burning beauty I remembered from the days of my childhood. I stood on the bridge a minute or two, gazing into that sunlight, and found a silent voice within me praying, 'Please, God, protect Marius and his child.'

I smiled at my own hypocrisy. I did not believe in any gods. I had placed my faith in the new nation, yet, after all these years, I was asking help from the God I had denied. What hypocrisy! But my mind – or was it my heart only? – kept repeating the prayer like a talisman.

I walked on quickly past Gervase's Rights of Man Café, and around the corner into my street. When I reached my room I threw off my pelisse and the bonnet that had been so much knocked about, and went to my little table to write that all-important note that I devoutly hoped would save the Redons from the conspirators in the Rue St Honoré.

I made no apologies. Marius Redon would despise them. Besides, there were much more important matters. The letter began, therefore, with a precise detailing of the events in the Luxembourg Gardens, followed by my visit to Sylvie's lodgings and everything that happened there. I gave very little rein to my suspicions, merely quoting the remarks which, in my view, denoted the intention of murdering Marius Redon if he did not die in the natural course of his lung injury. I ended with the instructions that I must place myself in readiness to leave Paris with Linette on Christmas morning.

I completed the letter simply with my signature, making no suggestions or interpretations. I felt this was my only hope for the Redons to use me in some way to aid them. After my uneasy return home from the Hôtel Dieu the previous night, I made certain now that I would return earlier tonight by leaving for the hospital considerably before my usual dinner hour.

I need not have concerned myself about the hour. When I reached the Hôtel Dieu I had my usual trouble in entering the hospital. An ancient veteran who had been with the Marquis de Montcalm at the fall of French Canada guarded the doors. 'Citizeness, there is no admittance. You have the pledge of Jacques-Louis Simon upon it. The Defence of Quebec for our great Marquis was not held more firmly.'

I could not stop myself from retorting, 'Firmly or not, you lost Quebec, Citizen Soldier!' It was a perfect way to lose any chance of winning him over. I stood as tall as I could and called over his head, hoping my voice would carry to someone who knew the nun, 'Sister Magdalen! Sister! May I see you?'

After a couple of minutes I began to wonder what I could do next. The only possibility was to wait near the hospital until I was permitted to enter. If all else failed, I determined to try that dreadful lower floor again, where the bodies were briefly kept. But as I was about to leave in bitter discouragement, a female voice called to the door-keeper who signalled to me with resignation, 'You are awaited, Citizeness.'

I hurried past him into the building. The straw pallets had been thrown upon the floor for the night, the beds were set up in row upon row against the walls, and the steamy odour of cabbage soup assaulted my nostrils. A young, ethereal nun motioned to me with one long fragile forefinger.

'Please to wait, Mademoiselle. Sister Magdalen is busy at the moment but she will pass this way shortly.'

I waited, grateful for the opportunity, and when the evening meal arrived, I was glad to assist in delivering the bowls of soup in which large chunks of bread were soaking. Then Sister Magdalen arrived, looking tired and strained. There were stains the colour of dried blood upon her knuckles.

'I am happy to see you, Mademoiselle. I learned today from Mademoiselle Linette's story that you are suddenly much mistrusted by the Redons. I hope you can reassure me.'

'I can do nothing, Sister, except to swear that I was innocent of that affair in the Gardens. But I have a letter which must be delivered to Captain

82

Redon. It is urgent. Sister – ' I caught her wavering, tired eyes. 'Of the utmost urgency!'

She shook her head. Again there was the suggestion of discouragement and defeat. 'Impossible, Mademoiselle. Monsieur Marius has had a very bad attack. The wound and then the exertion, you know. I have just come from his bedside. He regained consciousness, I am thankful to say, but is now asleep.'

I leaned against a partition and tried not to let the sickness of despair make me forget that other danger he faced. 'Will he recover, do you think?'

She passed a shaking hand over her eyes.

'Who can say? What do surgeons know? They are as ignorant as nurses. It seemed to me that his exertions had made him stronger, but all the same, he is only just recovering from a severe attack. I do believe his notion of removing from his bed was a good one. It was only the fantastic exertion at the house where he found his daughter. And then the long walk back. He was right, though, in theory.' She studied my face, understood my own emotions, which she obviously shared. 'We must pray for him.'

Beyond prayer I scarcely knew what to do after her dreadful news.

'Yes, Sister. But if – when he awakens, will you be certain that he reads this letter?'

'Your apology?' she asked with the faintest note of sarcasm.

'No. Whether he believes I intended Linette to be taken by force today matters very little. But he must understand that the information in this letter is the truth.'

She took my folded paper between her thumb and forefinger.

'Very well. I believe you. I will do what I can when he awakens.'

83

'Thank you. I will wait to hear from him, or from you. He must tell me what I am to do. And, Sister, if you value his life, let no one see him or Linette when you are not present. His life is also in danger from hired assassins.'

She seemed to sense I spoke the truth. She inclined her head, and I left. When I reached my lodgings I found that the mail from the south, from Lyon and the Swiss cantons, had arrived that day, for the man and wife who owned my building had picked up a letter for me at the central receiving station. I recognised the writing; I had finally heard from Paul. My own letter to him was still unfinished on my table. I hurried up the stairs to my room, dropped my reticule and bonnet, and broke the seal of Paul's letter.

My dearest little girl . . .

It was hard to believe I had once been profoundly moved by being called Paul's 'little girl.'

How long it is since I stood before you, touched that long chestnut curl which nestled so charmingly!

Trust Paul not to mention that the curl had nestled on my bosom. It no longer did so. I wore my hair free and rather thick to my shoulders in the back and a trifle shorter about my face. Neither breasts nor limbs nor any of the anatomy between had ever existed for Paul and me. Paul was highly proper. Sylvie had once said jokingly that the Swiss cantons were ideal for Paul, he was so very Calvinistic and so very unlike his earthy French forebears.

I take pen in hand to relate a delightful idea that has occurred to a great lady of my acquaintance. If you will oblige the Principessa Visconti in the most pleasant way – it involves a highly scenic journey over the Alpine passes – we shall be united at last, and I may see you long before we might have expected to meet.

How pompous it sounded!

I am persuaded Sylvie will behave in her usual addlepated fashion, but I suggest that you heed the instructions of Her Highness and do not hesitate to accept any largesse; for this great lady is more than generous.
Until we meet then, let me close now with all the long suppressed affection of your own,

Paul Vallier.

So he was urging me to trust the Visconti woman. But then, Paul had never been a very penetrating observer of humanity. I thought I could see from this letter that he was innocent in making his suggestion that I oblige the principessa. He did not even know that large sums were being offered me to co-operate in taking a child from her father, much less that they had hinted at murdering the father. However Paul might have changed, he would never condone murder.

I was considering what to reply to the address he gave in Geneva when I heard footsteps on the stairs. The steps of a lightweight person, but there was no mistaking the squeak of that stair halfway up from the landing. I went to the door, hoping against all common sense that this was a messenger from the hospital, to assure me that Marius Redon would receive me tonight. Instead, as I opened the door, I saw the black-clad little man, Ridetti, with one thumb of each gloved hand stuck in his pockets.

'The payment in earnest of your good faith,' he rattled off, obviously obeying his order with care.

While I stared, wondering what I should do with it, I received a small leather bag which contained silver coins newly minted of France, and coins of Geneva and Milano. I was still fingering these uncertainly when he handed me a smaller bag with similar drawstrings. This bag contained gold coins of several denominations and several countries, including some very old ducats of Milano itself.

'But what am I to do with them?' I asked in a tone that even I recognised as plaintive.

'I am told to inform you that you have carried out your first mission. You have established a new relationship with the man in the Hôtel Dieu. You are to carry out the plan discussed with Her Highness. *Au revoir,* Mademoiselle.'

'Farewell,' I corrected him, wishing this might be the last time we met, but doubting it all the time.

He acted as though he had not heard me and went rapidly down the stairs and out into the darkness. I think the two bags of coins troubled me less than the knowledge that my every move after my departure from Sylvie's lodgings had been faithfully reported to the Principessa Visconti.

As I got my heavy winter cloak out of the armoire before going to a small supper at Gervase's café, I told myself that I was foolish to have been surprised that Ridetti had followed me. Ridetti or another of the principessa's hirelings. She certainly would not stop at employing one rascal when two or more would suit her purposes. I therefore determined to enjoy myself at the café. I refused to spend the time haunted by the conviction that Marius and his daughter would never yield in their hatred of me.

I entered the café quietly, took the table in one far corner where I could sit on the small, uncomfortable settee against the wall and be served without causing too much attention from Gervase's livelier patrons. Gervase himself came over to polish my table with his dirty cloth and to ask me, grinning widely, 'And have you succeeded in obtaining the post with the old harridan?'

I was amused at this all too common picture of the formidable principessa. 'Yes, I am happy to say. I do wish I had been told that Ridetti was going to snatch up that wretched child in the Gardens today. Then I shouldn't have been so indignant with my poor friend Sylvie. I thought it very brave of Ridetti to do such a thing in full view of the world, so to speak.'

Gervase shrugged. 'Put a knife to her ear, I understand. The child went along with him. Then, at the house in St Honoré, the girl screamed and kicked and behaved like a hoyden. Then the father came storming in and afterward, a whole company of soldiers.'

'Not a company. Three.'

Gervase leaned over me a little too closely. 'The princess is not too nice in her habits. Shouldn't be necessary to threaten a child with a knife. Much better for a kindhearted young lady like yourself to take the child.'

'Thank you,' I said, carefully adding, 'but I cannot allow you to criticise the princess. She is my employer now, you know.' Let him repeat that to his master! Or to be more precise, his mistress!

I ate a hot supper which proved to be a tasty pot-au-feu, wonderful on a cold night. I ordered only what I could afford, although Gervase managed to be excessively generous and by the time I left his café I had eaten a healthy meal more suited to dinner than supper. Gervase had many excuses for accompanying me to my lodgings, but I refused them all. Any friendship that I formerly felt for

Gervase disappeared the moment I knew he had been purchased by the principessa.

Ignoring his other patrons, Gervase went with me to the street, protesting his affection and adding that if I married him, I might sink my reward from the principessa into the café.

'Then I can enlarge it. Purchase that old fool's building next to mine—'

Ruthlessly, I cut into his dreams. 'But of course it will be tedious. A journey so far as Italy. A pity I cannot deposit the child somewhere less distant than the plains of Lombardy. Then I could return to Paris and my friends.'

Would he take the bait and tell me if any harm toward Linette was planned on the journey?

He was all enthusiasm. 'But how simple then!' I thought he would go on pouring out these sinister hints, but he was suddenly tongue-tied and I looked around for the cause. I saw no one who looked suspicious but the square was busy enough so that he could have seen anyone. I took his partial confession to be a very strong hint that some evil might be intended for Linette as well as for her father.

I slept restlessly that night, wondering what I would do if the Redons continued to mistrust me and refused to heed my warnings. Perhaps then I might convince Sister Magdalen of the principessa's immediate plans. Almost satisfied by this solution, I closed my eyes.

By the early morning light things looked even gloomier. I was so busy trying to think of what I would do if the nun failed me too, that I missed the waterseller when he came through our street with his yoked water jugs. He did awaken me by crying his wares, however, and by the time I reached Gervase's café for breakfast, I was in a more cheerful frame of mind.

I had begun to drink my chocolate, foaming and hot, comforting on a thick, grey December day, when Gervase came to hang about my chair, leaning over like a playful bear in his attempt to, as he put it, steal a kiss. I was so busy thinking over various plans to aid the Redons in escaping their fate that I scarcely troubled to fend him off.

'Gervase, do be sensible. You know quite well I am betrothed. It would be highly improper if I were to encourage another man's attentions.'

'A poor stick of a man! Forget him.'

'On the contrary. A very solid, big man, as big as you. And a soldier. That is . . . Paul was once a soldier.'

'Bah! That one! A traitor to the Republic. Did he not desert our armies when they were losing? He deserves no consideration, none of such devotion.' He tried to kiss my cheek just inside the deep brim of my bonnet and I twisted away impatiently. But it was not my gesture that made him raise his head and stand stupefied, staring at someone who had just entered his café.

I glanced over at the closing door and saw Sister Magdalen looking her usual imperturbable self, but apparently an odd sight to Gervase's patrons. Since the Revolution, when all priests and nuns had to swear allegiance to the constitution, there had been few cassocks or habits seen on the streets. The non-juring religious community had fled long ago, but I knew Sister Magdalen, being a practical woman, had taken the oath and remained where she could do the most good.

I suspected she was here with good news. I certainly hoped so, for she would not come this far to tell me the Redons refused to see me again. But to Gervase her presence was a complete shock. He behaved like a little boy caught with his hand in the poor box. He had almost leaped away from me, not an easy task for one so big.

'Sister? You've come to collect for the poor? I am a poor man myself. Business is terrible—' A flicker of a smile passed over Sister Magdalen's face. The little café was almost filled and the steam of many breaths registered already on the long window overlooking the Place Michel. Gervase caught that faint reaction and added hurriedly, ' – except for breakfast. But all the same, let me contribute a few sous. Some assignats. Yes. I'll get you some assignats.'

'Excellent!' the nun agreed. 'We can use any contributions at the Hôtel Dieu. But I have actually come with a message for Mademoiselle Dubeque.'

I almost laughed at Gervase's volunteering money before it was asked, but I started to rise as the Sister crossed between the table to me. As usual, I could not guess from her demeanour the message she carried for me.

'Will they see me?' I blurted out almost before she took the chair opposite me.

'They will.'

'Then they forgive me? Sister, they must have forgiven me. I knew nothing of the attempt on Linette. I swear to you—'

She raised her hand, effectively cutting off my outburst, as she reminded me, 'It is not for me to forgive you. You have not offended me. Nor do I mistrust you. As to the feelings of Captain Redon and his daughter, I cannot speak for them. I know only that Monsieur has asked to see you. He read your letter with great care. Has read it a number of times. If you satisfy him as to your capability, you are to leave Paris tonight in disguise.'

'What! But that is impossible. So soon! And where am I to go?'

Sister Magdalen rose. 'Come with me now. I

90

know nothing of your objections. You must arrange them with Monsieur Marius.'

'Yes, yes, of course.'

I started out with her at once but it was disconcerting to see Gervase wink broadly at me as I passed him, and whisper, 'You are doing splendidly.' I was much relieved to realise that he could not have overheard us, but out on the street I explained to her, 'He is one of them. Sometimes it seems the whole world is in the principessa's pocket.'

'Not quite!' said Sister Magdalen firmly, and much encouraged by her confidence, I matched my steps to hers and walked rapidly toward the Cité bridge and the Hôtel Dieu.

Tonight . . . I was to leave tonight, but disguised as what? And where was I to go?

CHAPTER SEVEN

'THEN Captain Redon is somewhat recovered? That is wonderful news.'

Sister Magdalen agreed. 'He is in particularly good spirits since the post came. A letter he had been awaiting, which gave him excellent news from the south. And that, along with a good night's sleep and some exercise this morning, has put him in high spirits. Naturally, he does too much, but then, that is his way.'

A letter which gave him excellent news. Anyone as attractive as Marius Redon was sure to have women who wrote to him, and of course, receipt of such news would cheer him. I was astonished at my own reactions to such a possibility. I found myself violently jealous. What an absurdity, when I scarcely knew the man and was reasonably sure he despised me! Besides, he was a widower and a soldier. He had many acquaintances, no doubt half of them women.

When I reached the hospital in Sister Magdalen's company, it was surprising how easily we reached Marius Redon's little cubicle. Sister Magdalen called to him but there was no answer. We both looked around then and saw him across the wide hall with Linette, staring out through the aperture of a long medieval 'light,' a window crowded high with old furniture and debris. He saw us then and signalled to the nun with that rare, warm smile I had seen once or twice. Other patients were walking or stumbling about with the aid of sticks, but there was the usual long row of beds and cots whose occupants either stared up at the roof or watched the hall's activities with interest.

Sister Magdalen went to Marius in her usual confident way and I followed, trying to reveal no excitement, no anxiety, trying to behave with the calm, dispassionate sense of the letter I had written to him.

'Forgive my not receiving you as a proper host,' he told us with light irony. But he spoke almost entirely to the nun. 'This pillar is extraordinarily comfortable and I don't like to leave it.'

'You are doing very well,' Sister Magdalen told him calmly. 'You have been walking about and standing now for more than an hour. You would do well to return to your bed, Monsieur.'

'I told him so. I told him!' Linette put in. 'Papa, please!'

Marius absently stroked her soft, flyaway brown hair.

'Yes, I know. Later. But there is so much to do first. Citizeness Dubeque, we have decided to trust you.' No longer was it the daringly friendly 'Clare' but I was grateful for any favours. 'If their plan is to send Linette and you to Italy at Christmas, we must forestall them.'

'I will leave you three to plan,' said Sister Magdalen, but Marius gestured to her with his free hand.

'No, Sister, you are especially needed.'

Now I was jealous of a nun, a friend who had helped me, beside all else! However, I retained a coolness I was far from feeling. I became distinctly aware of Marius' frequent glances at me during the course of our planning but I retained the façade of calm, correct interest in a position for which I was applying.

Marius shifted his position against the pillar. Obviously he was tired, but it was equally obvious that he was stronger than he had been two days ago. I was immensely relieved.

'If Citizeness Dubeque agrees, she will escort my daughter to her inheritance in Italy.'

'I should like to know a little more about what I am doing. You know I have been approached by the principessa, and yet I am to take your daughter to Milano.'

'I have my reasons.'

'It is all very mysterious. I suspect the princess is anxious to put Linette on the road to Italy in order to cause some apparently reasonable accident. But the money belongs to Linette at this minute, doesn't it?'

'Not until she reaches Milano and is vouched for by the banking house of Galliotto-Molinari with her Uncle Bernardo as witness. Bernardo has been an invalid for years, but we were once comrades together.'

I wondered at this picture of the sinister Bernardo Visconti. Marius saw him in quite a different light.

'And you have almost nothing to say about your daughter's wealth?'

'At the time of the prince's death three months ago, I was already wounded, and it was supposed that I would die. Provision had to be made for Linette's guardianship in that event.'

'What a greedy person the princess must be!' I remembered her dry, tightening fingers. She was not a woman to let go of anything she had once touched.

The Captain did not deny this, but he explained the circumstances. 'She has a fondness for several adopted relations, I believe. Descendants of her late brother.'

I looked around, lowered my voice, and mentioned what seemed to me almost as important a problem as getting Linette to Milano. 'But once Linette reaches Milano and is acknowledged the heiress, what is to prevent the princess from attempting her death?'

He smiled with a hint of mischief. 'I shall suggest her inheritance go to the Church or to the poor, something of that sort, in the event of her death while underage. The old harridan would find it difficult to win a legal war against the Church so close to Rome. Besides, she cannot live forever, and without the princess, her relations have no claim upon Linette's estate.'

I only hoped he was right. Bringing the matter back to the immediate problem, I said, 'Sister Magdalen mentioned that we were to leave tonight. Our places on the Lyon Diligence must be booked. It is a very popular run.'

'They have been booked. We have our good Sister to thank for that. But you will appear to be travelling alone when you take your seat. And disguised.'

Sister Magdalen added, 'Otherwise, my having purchased the booking would have been pointless. You will leave Paris as Sister Magdalen of the Hôtel Dieu.'

For once I was speechless.

Marius was amused at my reaction. 'Will you find it so difficult to live up to this lofty image? When you have passed the last barrier beyond the Mont Cenis pass and the Italian border, you may return to your charming self.'

'But Linette?'

'All that will spin itself out. It is better that you do not know. Then we cannot accuse you falsely again.'

I could no longer contain my curiosity about another crucial factor.

'What of your own danger here in Paris? Have you considered that? She hates you, and I feel sure she would contrive your death.'

He paid no attention whatever to this reasoning. It disturbed me because everything I had said was perfectly true. However, I was here to oblige him and his daughter in any way possible. Perhaps the letter he received today 'from the South' was from Italy. It had prompted him to immediate action. I did not doubt now that he was keeping many secrets about this trip from me. I would not care if I could be certain he and his daughter would be safe. In that moment I swore privately to do all that was possible to protect Linette, but I was haunted by the great danger Captain Redon faced after we had gone.

Meanwhile, he soothed me with the very specious remark, 'All will go well, providing you keep secret only the fact that you are leaving tonight, and in what guise. Otherwise, they will expect you to report to them. You might write them a note and have it delivered, explaining that I have agreed you may take the child at Christmas. Say that I have relapsed, or am on the verge of death.'

'You very nearly were last night,' Sister Magdalen reminded him but I could see that he did not like to remember that so I simply agreed to all he said. He was looking considerably paler than when we met a few minutes before and I guessed this interview had overtaxed him. At the same time, not wanting to stare at him, I glanced around at the other patients and the healthy citizens that I took to be visitors. I may have been oversensitive to the danger, but I did fancy that a stout market woman visiting her husband seemed more interested in our group than in him.

I said softly to Captain Redon, 'I have no doubt she has spies here. Perhaps it would be well to play a little comedy for their benefit, if I am to report that you are dying.'

'Bravo, Citizeness!' he congratulated me with a sparkle of humour and probably with little dramatic ability necessary, he staggered against the pillar and was helped to his little cubicle by his daughter and Sister Magdalen. With infinite relief he stretched out on his cot and then lay there, regarding us with arms crossed behind his head.

'Are we all letter-perfect?' he asked us.

I said, 'When shall I change, and where? And how am I to disappear without her spies wondering? They must watch my lodgings.'

'Very true,' the sister agreed. 'And on no account must Mademoiselle Clare be seen on the streets after the shops are shuttered late in the evening. It would be certain to arouse attention. However, I am often out at midnight on errands of one sort or another.' We knew they must be errands of mercy but did not mention the fact.

'But the Lyon stage leaves anywhere from two to four in the morning,' Linette put in. 'You said so yourself, Sister.'

Captain Redon agreed. 'A maddening schedule, but we have accounted for that. Our Clare will arrive at the Hôtel de Sens where the coach takes up its waybill a few minutes before two.' At least, by a slip of the tongue, he had called me Clare.

'She will appear to be Sister Magdalen. Our real Sister will have returned home with you tonight after your visit to the hospital and will remain in your lodgings until morning, leaving you to depart in her place. I suspect she has not slept in twenty-four hours, thanks to my activities yesterday, so this will give you a chance to recover, my dear Sister.'

'And we will bring with us another habit into which you will change at your lodgings,' the Sister finished before holding both palms up and saying lightly, 'It will be quite simple.'

'But Linette!' I exclaimed, baffled by all this Machiavellian plotting.

The three of them grinned at me as if they were one conspirator. Linette hastened to reassure me. 'That's the amusing part. Wait and see.'

I did not press the matter. 'And will I know what to do with this young lady when I reach Milano?'

'All taken care of,' Marius said.

It was certainly mysterious, but if it defeated the principessa's ugly plans, I didn't care whether the Redons trusted me or not. Well, perhaps I cared, but my own emotions were not nearly so important at the moment as saving the lives of this stubbornly determined pair. Once the situation had been explained to me, it was clear that I was no longer needed, so I started to leave, hoping against all my feeble hopes, that I would be called back. I was, but not in order to be thanked or to receive a flash of Marius Redon's charm.

'Sister Magdalen will see you here this evening.'

'And I will walk back to your lodgings with you at that time,' the nun reminded me. 'Then Sister Magdalen – you, this time – will return to the hospital until time to depart for the Hôtel de Sens and the Lyon Coach. Trust me to make my way back to the hospital tomorrow morning, in my own way. I had a deal of practice during the Revolution when the churches were proscribed.'

I asked nothing further. Let them work out their plans together. I felt that in spite of their protests, none of them trusted me fully, and it was vastly unfair of them.

'Very good. And Sister, I shall leave in my rooms the two little packets of coins sent to me by the principessa. Give them to your poor. I shall see you this evening then, Sister.' I added coldly to the Redons who were watching me with intensity, 'I will send a message to the principessa, saying that you have had a relapse and that I will remove Linette to the Lyon coach on Christmas morning. Good day.'

No one called me back until I had passed beyond the crimson drape. In my fancy, I thought I heard Marius Redon's voice call my name, but there was no repetition and I went out of the hospital, well aware that any of the eyes watching me curiously throughout the hospital itself might belong to one of the principessa's hirelings. To make certain they believed us about the Captain's condition, I made a little show of dabbing at my eyes.

I found myself excessively nervous throughout that tense and all-important day. I felt that I could not bear to face the dreadful people at the house in the Rue St Honoré so I wrote a note to them and went to Gervase to have it delivered rather than wait for the regular city post which would carry it across the Seine within the afternoon. But if Gervase sent a boy from his kitchen, the whole matter would be settled in half an hour.

In Gervase's café I wrote my note. I began by thanking Sylvie for having introduced me indirectly to the charm of poor Captain Redon and his sweet, intelligent daughter.

'I had originally hesitated to assist Her Highness, as you are aware, Sylvie, because I felt that our action in removing the child from her father would be cruel, but today, his second collapse in twenty-four hours, told me that it would be grossly wrong to leave the child permanently in his care for he will certainly be gone before Christmas. Therefore, you need have no concern for the father. I am making plans, wooing the child's trust, and will see her again this evening. At that time, I trust I will have finally convinced her that her great-grandmother is only acting in the girl's best interests.

'I was persuaded to this end by a letter I have received at long last from Paul. He advises me to oblige the princess and naturally, his wishes have been mine for many years.'

That last line was true. The fact that Sylvie would make false assumptions did not trouble me. She had allowed herself to be used by criminals, and I could never trust her again.

I closed with a mention of the money Ridetti had delivered to me.

'Many thanks to Her Highness for her generosity. You may advise her that the money will be devoted to the best advantage possible.'

This amused me and I signed with a flourish, sanded and sealed the letter, and sent it off with the eager co-operation of Gervase.

'So you've actually taken the post! Excellent! It will serve you well,' and Gervase went on at length about the profitable future which would result from my accepting the principessa's money. I could not fail to be aware that Gervase included himself in this delightful picture. Undoubtedly he would do me the honour of marrying me, once I had carried out Her Highness' scheme and received my full payment. His thoughts were so obvious that I laughed in his face, but he chose to read my amiability as encouragement.

Having settled the matter, I returned to my lodgings and tried to imagine how I would make a trip over the Alpine passes while carrying no more luggage than I could take in a reticule hidden in the skirts of a nun's habit. I thought so much about the ridiculous Comédie Française aspect of my trip that by the time evening came and I was on my way to the Hôtel Dieu, I had worked myself into a kind of silent, stubborn resentment. I was putting myself into discomfort and danger for no better reason than the charm of a man I scarcely knew, and even that had been directed away from me. He had shown me precious little gratitude today.

Now, of course, I cared about saving two human lives that had been threatened in my presence, but I thought the Redons at least owed me their thanks, and perhaps a smile to indicate trust. I was being altogether absurd.

At the hospital entrance I was pleasurably surprised to meet Linette, who said she had been on the watch for me. She then turned a lugubrious face to me, and whispered, 'I am playacting. Papa has been so improved. He rested for a time then exercised inside that dreadful little room of his, but Sister and I have pretended he was frightfully ill. We pull long faces and even put our sleeves to our eyes now and again.'

I caught the hint and set my own face in similar lines, very like one of those absurd masks of tragedy, I daresay. But I was immensely cheered by the girl's reception of me which seemed to put me in her good graces again, and by the news that her father's health was improving.

We made our way above stairs where I found myself amazingly nervous, trying to recall all the things I must do before I was safely past the Paris barriers, and wondering where I would find Linette on the trip. Surely, she would not be sent by some other method the entire distance to Lyon. For one thing, I was fairly certain her father could not afford it. He didn't appear to be a man of wealth, or he would not have been relegated to the Hôtel Dieu as a patient. On the other hand, he had not tried to seize his daughter's inheritance. But perhaps he intended to use it once she was safely in Milano. To do that he must follow. Was this one of his secret plans? What a glorious miracle if he actually succeeded in recovering and made his way to Milano!

Sister Magdalen was excited. She managed very well outwardly, but within, I guessed the nervousness that filled me and the carefully concealed joy in Linette's eyes were contagious. The good Sister's hand shook as she beckoned me to the crimson drape that provided some privacy for Marius Redon.

Inside the cubicle Marius sat on the edge of the cot, carelessly, without the coat he had worn earlier. His shirt was open at the throat, his cravat removed. He kept making unconscious gestures of loosening his shirt at the throat and I suspected he was not feeling as well as he pretended, and was having difficulty breathing. But I tried not to let him see my concern.

He stood up, bent slightly over my hand like a beau of the Old Regime, and then held my fingers as if he had forgotten them while we talked. I did not wish to remind him, for I was intensely aware of his warm pressure upon that hand.

'Lovely Citizeness Clare. You bring something very special to this hellhole.'

'Merely my perfume, I expect, Citizen,' I said but he must have read something in my manner, for he smiled.

'Yes, probably. When Linette is eighteen you must introduce her to that particular perfume.'

So he thought I might be acquainted with the Redons six years from now! I found it wonderfully reassuring, but one look at Marius Redon's tired eyes reminded me that it was a dream.

'Have you notified the old harridan that you will be able to remove Linette for the Alpine trip at Christmas?'

'I have done so. I also received two little packets of coins, silver and gold. Perhaps I should take them for use on the journey, but I don't like to do so. I prefer that Sister Magdalen take the money for the hospital since I shall not actually be earning it for the principessa.'

'I prefer to have you use my money on the journey,' Marius said calmly.

He repeated the brief instructions, although I understood them quite well. I did not understand how I would help the Redons, except as a decoy, by taking a place on the Lyon Coach disguised as a nun, with no Linette in sight. However, they all seemed to know what they were doing; so I must rely upon these three unlikely plotters.

When Sister Magdalen thought it time to leave for my lodgings and what I regarded as the first step of our plot, I found my knees quaking. Fortunately, two petticoats and the russet gleam of my silk skirts managed to hide this dreadful attack of nerves. And fear? I had no fear for myself yet, but I feared strongly for the Redons.

'You will return here once you have become Sister Magdalen,' Marius instructed me, adding as if impatient with himself, 'I'm sorry. Please forgive me. I am not at my best. It's been a long day. I meant to say, "Would you please return here?" From here you will seem to have been called away on an errand of mercy. You will order a horse and a closed carriage and set out for some address on the Right Bank in the Marais. Once you have reached the Marais Quarter, change your mind and ask to be deposited at the Hôtel de Sens.' He stopped. We all waited expectantly. His wary little smile appeared again, tired but authentic. If it had an ironic curve, the irony was aimed at himself. 'Again, I should say, if it pleases you.'

I looked down at my hand in his. 'It does, Citizen.' It was as far as I could go and as a matter of truth, it was further than I should go and remain a decently reared female. How odd and out of fashion that sounded in my thoughts! After the convulsion of the past ten years, females reared in the old way were almost an anachronism.

When I released my slightly numb fingers from his, I noted, 'Your strength is improving, Citizen. You will outlive the principessa by a score of years.'

He laughed and Sister Magdalen said, 'I devoutly pray you are right.'

But Linette reminded us that we were supposed to be sad, and we became suitably grave as we went outside the curtain and made our way through the hall where the patients were being made ready for the night. Sister Magdalen stopped by a number of beds on our way out, and when we reached the Left Bank it was past midnight.

'It should be easier to see if we are followed,' I suggested, as my companion frowned up at the starry sky. My fingers felt stiff with the cold, possibly because of my exceeding anxiety.

In answer to my observation, Sister Magdalen remarked with the common sense she always displayed, 'We must assume they are watching us. We are going to this elaborate charade for their benefit.'

'But after I have gone, and in one of your habits – ' I didn't like to ask where this habit was at the moment ' – how will you, this second Sister Magdalen, leave my lodgings tomorrow?'

'My child, I am a conspirator of long practice. You forget that there was a time when all who wore my habit were in daily fear of being hanged from those lamp posts. During the September Massacres, for example, I had been doing what I could among the prisoners at St-Germain-des-Prés. I escaped into a well, through a cellar, and came out upon a rooftop. One never knows when one's ingenuity will be needed.'

I looked at her with admiration. She appeared to be her placid self, but I did think she was a trifle less calm than she pretended. When we reached my lodgings I started to say good night, then made a pretence of asking her to stop for a glass of wine. She agreed and came up.

Once inside my room and having examined all of it, including the tiny rooftop balcony, we went about our business. To my astonishment she wore two habits with extra bandeaux and headpieces and even two crucifixes. She stripped off one and suggested I wear it over my own gown. All my hair was bundled under the coif and I scarcely knew myself in the slightly unsilvered mirror I had used for years. The head covering was soiled, slightly wrinkled, but worse had been seen in the city streets during the last few years. No one, seeing my face with its hazel eyes and full mouth, would ever mistake it for the high-boned, austere features and blue eyes of Sister Magdalen, but my clothing should be enough to allay suspicion.

I felt bundled to death as we said our good-byes and wished each other 'God be with you,' but fortunately it was a cold December night and even regular clothes plus a nun's habit were not too much protection. She had been wearing borrowed shoes, because her order had not provided for her in any way since she had sworn allegiance to 'The French Republic One and Indivisible' as it was phrased; so I retained my own slippers with their slightly higher heels, which brought me to her height.

As I stepped out into the street, thankful for the folds of cloth that prevented my face from being seen, I started to walk in my own fashion, then remembered and began to imitate Sister Magdalen's firm stride. At the Pont au Double I was accosted by a dark creature creeping out of the slime under the bridge.

'Alms, good Sister, for the love of God!'

I thought it would not be very clever of me to

open my reticule, thus letting him know I had more than one or two sous, so I pointed to the looming Cathedral of Notre Dame among the medieval shacks and hovels. I also remembered to bless him, and then I strode on, my many skirts flapping against my limbs. The poor fellow seemed to be harmless. He started off for Notre Dame while I crossed to the Hôtel Dieu.

In the hospital I could not possibly be Sister Magdalen, even though the lighting was now reduced to the obscurity of a few candles; so I became a sister of a silent order and managed to remain in shadow, exhibiting only my fingers to bless a patient, and a mischievous, black-haired boy who called to me on the lower floor, but I tried not to make any worse blasphemy of the good sister's work.

I saw no sign of Linette. I approached the crimson drape of Captain Redon's temporary home and was not accosted by any of the patients. There was that now familiar and dreadful cacophony of groans and the murmurs of those who talked in their sleep, but I gritted my teeth and tried not to think of that suffering since I could do nothing to aid anyone until, and if, I returned from Italy.

Flattening my voice to Sister Magdalen's calm, un-emotional tones, I called his name.

'Enter.' There was such a long pause before he spoke, and in the most feeble way, that I pushed aside the drape and rushed in. 'Are you ill? Shall I fetch someone?' What a terrible thing that Sister Magdalen was not here! She would be certain to know what to do. I was met, however, by Marius Redon, fully dressed, leaning against the wall winking at me. I almost committed the folly of laughing.

'In heaven's name, do not stand on ceremony with me,' I insisted in an undervoice, motioning him to sit down.

He was amused at the aptness of my order and

agreed to do so if I would. We sat there looking at each other briefly. I would have given a good deal to know what he was thinking as he studied me in that unfamiliar habit and coif. My own thoughts were chaotic. I wondered most of all if I would ever see him again. In spite of all his bold pretences, I could see at close range that he was still a patient very much in danger. He looked more tense, as though he could use a good sleep of at least twelve hours. But he was determined to win this battle with the principessa.

I broke the silence that, in other circumstances, might have been happy and contented.

'You are wondering whether you dare trust me,' I guessed.

After a moment during which I thought he would jokingly deny this ugly truth, he asked with gentle sarcasm, 'Can I really know, until it is too late?' He shrugged. 'If I were to rely on my senses, I would have trusted you long ago. But that child's life is considerably more important than the fact that I find you physically desirable. That very desirability may be something the old woman has counted on.'

I must have looked a trifle flushed at this barbed compliment but I pretended a coolness that brought the present and its problems sharply back between us.

'Perhaps you would do well not to judge me until I have completed this fantastic scheme. So far as I can see, I depart from Paris, heavily disguised, and do not even escort the person most concerned in all this.'

He looked at me with more innocence than even his daughter could have mustered. 'But of course, you do. Be patient. If you are not aware of Linette's little joke, you will never again be suspected by harsh fellows like me.'

I did not understand this reference to Linette's 'joke' but I tried a weak smile which did not mirror my feelings. I resented this proof that I was once more being falsely accused. I started to rise. 'It must be half past one by now, Captain Redon. I would do well to—'

'At least . . . Marius.'

'Marius, I would do well to leave now.'

He took up my hand and I was giving serious consideration to forgiving him when he placed a number of large silver coins into my palm and closed my fingers over them. For an instant I felt like one of the females who paraded in the Palais-Royal and was furious with him, but it was a very natural gesture, since I had almost no money and was actually doing him a service.

He was sensitive enough to realise he had somehow insulted me. As he folded my fingers over the coins, he said quietly, 'I believe I know why you are helping us. You pity us and perhaps you like us. You could scarcely not like my little Linette. But we must be practical as well. I devoutly hope I do not die before I can carry out my part of our little conspiracy. But nothing is certain in this world; so you must be financially able to deliver Linette in safety, if I cannot.'

'But I know nothing of what we are to do once the coach comes down onto the Lombardy Plains.'

'That is all arranged, and Linette will know what to do.'

'Thank you. I am travelling in the dark. I understand.'

He looked as if he would like to say more, would like to trust me, but he did not yield. When I arose, he stood up and murmured, 'You are the loveliest Sister of Mercy I have ever encountered. Until we meet again . . . all my thanks. All my gratitude.'

This time he raised my clenched fist to his lips, then let me go.

I strode away in Sister Magdalen's fashion without looking back. I kept thinking, 'Is this the last time I will ever see him? Am I being used as a decoy for the entire Alpine journey? If so, I mean nothing to him.'

Resigned to this, but absolutely determined to cheat the principessa in her schemes, I stood outside the Hôtel Dieu for scarcely five minutes before coach wheels rattled over the cobblestones and I was provided with a dilapidated but perfectly efficient fiacre for the short journey to the Right Bank and the Marais Quarter, as I directed the crabbed and wrinkled coachman.

I followed Marius Redon's directions, first asking to be taken to the great house in the Marais called the Hôtel de Bourgogne, then, as we were actually approaching this town house, I changed my directions and told him to take me to the Hôtel de Sens.

'Ah! The Lyon Coach. Yes. You must run, Sister. It is leaving early tonight, to escape the clouds. Better weather for you tomorrow than for us Parisians, Sister.'

I did not reply. When I was set down at the ancient house, I went around to the coach yard, the inn yard as it must be called these days, and waited silently, trying not to move, as I had seen Sisters of Mercy stand so often in my youth. I recognised none of the other travellers gathered there, looking extraordinarily sinister under the high, eerie lantern-light. I began, surreptitiously, to examine them. Any one of the five gathered here might be agents of the principessa, but which of them? Meanwhile, I was very much aware of the close, curious regard of these five passengers. They had time to study me, as they awaited the putting

110

to of the team, and the loading of various boxes, packages, portmanteaux, even mail, although the regular mail service came by special coach these days, often with the first-priority military mail. If we had been travelling by the mail coach, I thought regretfully, we would have made far better time.

I soon realised I had been far too conscious of my own disguise, for these passengers proved to be transfers from the Calais Coach. They were Normans, Bretons, and a heavy, blond pair from the Lowlands. Once I began to make out individual conversations, I could see that I had nothing to fear from these people. They were clearly not Parisian. I relaxed with a long breath of relief.

CHAPTER EIGHT

THE great coach we were all expecting, which would accommodate more than a score of people, was not forthcoming. Complaints began among the passengers who were forced to stamp up and down in the cold night air to restore circulation, but a swaggering young postilion came by and announced with some satisfaction that if we intended to arrive at Lyon in decent time, that is to say, in less than five days, we would be taking the coach provided, an antiquated and springless affair which had been deemed too dilapidated to burn by revolutionary incendiaries.

'Our best diligence,' he explained, 'is on its way back from Lyon at this minute. It should be rattling past Melun in the morning. But tonight's coach will take up the lot of you and mayhap a few more on the imperial. Ay! On the roof,' he added, as he heard the groans among the men. 'There's the rooftop seats – on the imperial – for them as comes last.'

Our little group had been growing as he talked, and I watched them covertly. A mischievous child standing on a bench pulled on the rope that hoisted the lantern which illuminated the faces in the yard. Perhaps everyone resented this because it reminded us all of the many victims hanged to these lanterns during the bad days, but at this moment I was conscious only of the evil faces formed by the movements of that flickering light: hideous great noses, eyes sparkling with malice, long, cavernous mouths with canine teeth.

Everyone was so bundled against the cold that it was difficult to tell the males from the females, but I supposed it was the child's mother who slapped him noisily, and the lantern was replaced.

A great rattling of harness and hoofbeats sparking fire on the pebbled yard announced the arrival of the celebrated Lyon Coach. And a great disappointment it was, though the postilion had prepared us! The coach was a small affair, which boded ill for one's comfort on a long journey. Everyone stood aside politely after the steps had been let down, and I realised after an awkward moment that as Sister Magdalen, I was to be given the place of honour in the coach.

Feeling more and more sacrilegious – an odd sensation to one reared without religion – I inclined my head in gratitude, and stepped up into the carriage. I had no notion whether a true nun would take the choice seat on the right, facing forward, or would be self-sacrificing and choose another. Unlike the larger diligences on these routes, this coach did not have all seats facing forward, but I decided no one would expect me to sit with my back to the coachman and team, so I took the seat next to the window, but on the left side.

The interior of the coach rapidly filled and we were all startled when a tall, mustachioed soldier, one of the three in Captain Redon's company, crowded in among the other passengers and announced to me in a jolly voice,

'Here he is, Sister. My nephew. Your charge to Joigny. The rascal's mother and father will meet you. Here are his passport papers for the Paris barriers.'

Good Lord! I had no passport. Certainly no passport papers for Sister Magdelen! I sat up stiffly, earning an affronted look from the stout lady next to me. At the same time, I found the twelve-year-old 'boy' left here by the soldier now squeezing between the stout female and me. With his tousled, badly cut black hair and some sort of stain, walnut perhaps, on his skin to make him look swarthy, the boy left in my care looked astonishingly unlike Linette Redon, but I could not mistake the wink from her wise, almost adult eyes.

'You will be a good child, and no fussing,' I said sternly,when she persisted in wiggling her hips into that narrow space beside me, but she could see that I was amused. Almost at once, however, another danger presented itself. The boy, about seven or eight, who had been annoying us with the lantern rope, sat on his mother's lap across the coach and made some violent faces at Linette. Trouble would certainly come from that quarter because Linette, not to be outdone, promptly put her tongue out at the boy. I was amused but felt that such a sense of humour from a woman of the cloth would arouse curiosity, so I forced myself not to smile.

Besides, there was a more immediate problem to occupy my mind. As a local Parisian from the Hôtel de Sens bellowed out our departure and destination into the chill Paris night, the coach leaped forward, flinging us all backward, and we were off on the first step of our journey. We were also heading for the Paris barricades, and I had no passport. Would I be seized as a spy? God knows France had been attacked on all sides for eight years, and to the amazement and regret of other nations, had sent the Austrian, Prussian, and Russian armies scurrying back to their borders in full rout, but such a situation also meant danger at home, and our city barriers were as suspicious and complex as imperial border zones.

While I was considering what to do, and wondering if my robes would save me when added to what the entire coach had heard about Linette from the soldier, we rattled across Paris to what I supposed would be the barrier near the old gateway to the southeast. There were a few curious glances at me. Once it had been established that I was a nun, and one moving freely, they must have decided I had sworn allegiance to France, and was not an enemy; for the enemies on our borders were financially reinforced by the Church.

Small mundane conversations started up and occupied everyone except the boy across the carriage, twitching and constantly resetting himself on his mother's lap. During this time he managed to fix his bulging and slightly fishy eyes upon Linette who gave back as good as she got. Linette was a lean and very credible stripling in dark pantaloons tucked into boots just a trifle too big for her. She wore a dark brown coat with the tails abruptly cut away in front, in the mode of a year or two ago, and revealing her shirt frills as well as a waistcoat also somewhat large for her. Her white neckcloth must have been arranged in a hurry. It was ill tied and rapidly worsening, but I hoped this added to the look of a tousled, careless boy. Certainly her freckled nose and generally plain face did not give her sex away; yet it was an endearing face, asking few favours of life. I liked her more and more for her initiative and courage.

I felt it incumbent upon me as her saintly mentor to chide her as the other occupants of the coach saw her answer the boy with a particularly atrocious face, but I did not know the name under which she was travelling, and could only put my hand out as a warning to her. She grinned. She was enjoying herself enormously.

I took a greater interest in our fellow passengers during the minutes before we reached the barrier.

116

The stout woman and the man next to her were the Low Country people. They spoke in a strange, incomprehensible language and aside from rightfully resenting Linette's presence, they paid no attention to anyone else. Across the coach and tucking objects of food into various pockets in the leather lining of the seats were two men, probably Bretons, dark, square and forbidding, and then there was the woman between them who held the obnoxious child, but managed to twist around and drop a slab of cheese into what I at first believed was another pocket in the leather. I discovered after studying the slit for a minute or two, that this particular pocket was a tear in the aged, cracking leather. I smiled to myself, but I hoped she would locate the cheese later when she reached in and found it had very likely fallen down as far as the flattened leather on the seat.

The woman was not Breton, or in any case, she did not in the least resemble the men, and when she spoke to the mettlesome boy, it was a sharp, Parisian argot. Even more curious, she did not resemble her son in any way. She was blonde, with sharp, narrow features. The boy had a broad head, an unformed dab of a mouth, and eyes quite unlike the narrow blue eyes of his mother, if indeed she was his mother.

The idea startled me. Then I pretended to be sleepy and concerned with unwordly things, slipping the beads of my rosary through my fingers while I let my head fall back against the leather, my eyes half-closed. But beneath my lashes I watched the blue-eyed female. She did not behave suspiciously, but then, what agent worth her pay would do so?

Suddenly we came to a halt. We jolted back and forth, everyone fell into everyone else, and there was considerable commotion among the passengers unfortunate enough to be assigned places on the imperial of the roof. We all looked at each other, but I knew the first dangerous time had come. We were at the Paris barrier.

The coach door was swung open with authority. The head we saw there in the doorway did not reassure me. It was still wearing the great, mourning plume on the bicorne hat that I remembered from the days of the Revolutionary Convention and the Directory. The face beneath it was eminently suited to its job. There was intelligence, but little humanity, in that lean, hardboned face.

'Your papers, Citizens. File out.'

No one wanted to be first. They all looked at me. This time I could have done without their politeness. I hesitated, then got up with a rustling of all the clothing I wore. Linette jumped up. In a boyish voice she informed me, 'I can do it Sister. Remember, I have our papers.' We were now doubly illuminated, from the coach lamps and from the ruddy light of the lantern in the hand of the officer at the barrier.

We all filed out, climbing carefully down the steps that were unfolded. Linette helped me like a well-brought-up young lad doing his duty for a Sister of Mercy. The guard was obviously anti-clerical. He checked the papers of every other passenger before he came, at long last, to Linette and me.

'And you, Young Citizen. Let me see. Léon Trouville. So you travel with a religieuse, and yet you call yourself a loyal citizen of the Republic!'

Linette opened her mouth and started to protest, but I kicked her ankle lightly, and she subsided. The guard finally reached me.

'You, Citizeness Magdalen Marie Pelletier. The Republic has no need of Papists. Are you a non-juring sister?'

Linette, dancing up and down with anxiety,

pointed to something in the papers that apparently referred to me.

'No, Citizen. See? She has sworn. I can read it. She is loyal to the Republic.'

I nodded, gave him what I hoped was a 'loyal' look, and after studying the paper as if it were written in fire, he folded and returned it to me. He then staggered me by looking me up and down and remarking with a smirk, 'A pity, that profession of yours, Citizeness. You haven't the face for it.'

I didn't know whether to be insulted or amused but Linette clapped her hand over her mouth and I saw her eyes sparkling with laughter. I hustled her into the coach. Shortly afterwards, we rattled off down the ill-paved highway and into at least two or three hours of blackest night. I was too nervous to sleep for a time, after my nerve-racking encounter with the guardian of the barrier, but Linette fell asleep almost instantly, leaning against my shoulder. Poor lamb! She must have been exhausted after her long travail with her father.

Peculiarly enough, the bright eyes of the boy across the coach remained wide and watchful in a way I could only regard as sinister. Every time I tried to close my eyes, the boy's stare became fixed upon me. It was difficult to see anyone else in the coach during these hours, but the boy's eyes were always lighted, probably by the narrow band of lamplight that crept in through the ragged window coverings.

I must have napped after all. I do not recall the arrival of dawn but was awakened at a stop for one of the southbound posts, where the team was changed and the postilion came around to announce in his arrogant way that we might put up at the local inn for breakfast. I roused myself, feeling as if every muscle had been frozen into the twisted position I had taken during the long hours of immobility. But I was cheered by Linette's nudge in my ribs and her glance at the two passengers on our side of the coach. The stout lady and her husband were still snoring into each other's faces, both heads jauntily attired in tasselled nightcaps.

Linette giggled, and I very nearly did so. The Lowlanders had no difficulty the previous night with the sentinel of the barrier, so I assumed they spoke French, but this morning they were much too intent upon their sleep to bother with food as yet. The woman and child on the seats across from us had stepped down and gone into the desolate, godforsaken inn, and Linette and I followed. I devoutly hoped today was not a fast day in the religious calendar, for I was hungry and wanted my morning chocolate. If it was a fast day, it would affect none of these Republican French, but I would certainly seem a very odd kind of nun if I drank my rich, sugared chocolate.

The exterior was a poor excuse for an inn, bearing as it did a great resemblance to a stable, with clucking chickens strutting in and out, and the next team for the coach stamping uneasily in front of the only door. Linette was fascinated by the proud black and white hen, and said to me, 'I will never eat another chicken. I'd no notion they were so human.'

Nor did it help matters when we joined the other passengers at the long, rough table opposite the tap-room and were offered a chicken stewed with turnips and garlic for our breakfast. Linette was horrified, not over the menu but over the cannibalistic notion of eating her newfound friends, and this aroused some interest among the other diners. One of the Bretons said gruffly that this young lad was behaving in a chicken-hearted manner over chickens. Everyone laughed except Linette and then, remembering my habit, they all looked at me, for the most part apologetically.

The low-roofed, smoke-blackened room was very hot, thanks to the fire on the hearth, and when I was served a small bowl of strong coffee, I began to perspire. I thought of all the clothing I was wearing, an entire gown and petticoats beneath my habit, and sighed. I waited until the coffee was no longer steaming, and then drank it off.

I felt Linette's elbow in my side again and looked up, over the coffee bowl, intensely conscious of being watched. I might have known. Across the table the boy had fixed his unforgettable eyes upon me. I felt terribly certain that this intelligent child guessed I was a fraud, and probably knew why. I turned away from him, concentrated on my eggs, and hoped for the best.

Very soon, all my hopes in this direction were dashed. The nasty child began to stick his tongue out at Linette who took instant offence and returned the compliment. This apparently led to furtive hostilities which eluded the rest of us until we were leaving the table. The seven-year-old somehow got hold of a handful of Linette's hair and tugged hard. Linette let out an excessively feminine shriek. One of the rooftop passengers, a young fellow with a meek look and very nervous hands, stopped along with the obnoxious child's mother. They both stared at Linette.

Trying to mend things, I addressed Linette in my most soulful voice, 'My dear child, you must control these tantrums.'

Linette recovered but there was a gleam of revenge in her eyes as she agreed in her boyish voice, 'Ay, Sister!' But I looked away and carefully did not see the kick she gave to the boy's sturdy ankle. He let out a squawk or two and pretended to sob into his mother's skirts, but there were no tears when he got into the carriage. In a few minutes he was busy spreading a rip in the leather cushion behind his mother's back. It was the woman who troubled me now. She had begun to take a closer interest in Linette. Marius Redon's daughter was careful to sit with her right leg crossed over her left in male fashion. Except for that one betraying scream when her hair was pulled, she had done very well in her masquerade.

As we started up again, I realised the awful result of a garlic dish served to passengers tightly fitted into a small space. I nearly suffocated until other odours managed to subordinate the garlic. Whether these were an improvement, it would have been hard to say. The Lowlands family had removed their nightcaps, taken out bread, cheese and onions from the leather pockets of the coach and were now in the process of sharing the wine in a carafe between them.

After a few minutes of this public dining on a road that obviously had not been worked on since the forced peasant labour before the Revolution, another calamity threatened. Linette sat inhaling her neighbour's breakfast and rattling over wagon ruts half ice and half mud. As I was studying the hilly countryside, wondering if the intricate layers of clouds overhead meant rain, Linette pressed against my shoulder. 'I think I'm going to be ill.' She swallowed desperately. 'And I did want to be well when we see Father.'

Were we actually going to meet Marius Redon somewhere on the trip? 'Try hard dear!' I whispered, avoiding mention of her father. Then I remembered, a trifle late, that I was speaking to a boy. 'My dear Léon,' I added, aware that I had almost given away her sex to those sinister, staring eyes across the coach. 'Here, change places with me. Put your cheek against the cool leather.'

While the coach rolled and swayed, she managed to crawl over me and I shifted along the seat to be crowded in beside the lady Lowlander. Poor Linette pushed her face and both palms against the leather and did her noble best to fight off her motion sickness. I watched her anxiously. She felt for the handkerchief I offered. It was the only one I had bought, and she dabbed it nervously to her lips. Fortunately it was perfumed, and she managed with this scent to drive out the now stale odour of food.

In a valley between two sharply rising brown hills, we pulled up at a bridge. These planks over a meandering brook were examined to see if they would hold the weight of coach, passengers, and luggage, while the woman across the coach leaned forward to remind me unpleasantly, 'Your charge has a womanish weakness. I imagine you will be happy to see the last of the boy.'

'We must be charitable, Citizeness!' I murmured in the most maddeningly reproachful tones I could summon. 'The boy has been reared by his grandmother while his father marched in General Bonaparte's glorious armies,' I lied, trying to look saintly. 'The dear lady was so fond of Léon that I fear she kept him in petticoats too long, as they say.'

That ought to silence criticisms of Linette's lack of manliness.

Alas for plans and good intentions! Attempting to calm her embattled stomach, Linette looked out the window at the calm silvery stream, a branch of the beautiful Yonne River, and exclaimed enthusiastically, 'Oh, look Clare! We are in Burgundy! There to the east was a little stone with the post name.'

Everyone in the coach instantly stopped talking, chewing, or ruminating, and Linette blushed a deeper colour under the weathered look contrived by the walnut stain.

I said, 'My child, that is not good manners or respectful. You know how often your grandmamma

chided you. You must say Sister Magdalen Clare.'
I only prayed that no one remembered the name
read out on my passport by the guard at the barrier.

'Y-yes, Sister.' Then to change the subject, Linette
pointed out a gaggle of geese waddling along with
a wide expanse of feathered bottoms turned to us.
'But it is Burgundy, isn't it?'

'For some time now, I imagine. They say it is a
beautiful countryside in season.'

'And good food,' put in the Breton opposite
Linette. 'Always good food in Burgundy.'

The woman with the seven-year-old child cut in
sharply, 'You speak of it as in the Old Regime.
There are no provinces these days. This is probably
the Department of the Yonne River.'

Everyone looked guilty, as though the woman
carried a guillotine in her pocket. She seemed so
vehemently in favour of the Revolution that it did
not seem likely she was in the pay of the principessa,
but then, this might be her way of concealing
her real motives. I must suspect everyone. I was
glad of the discussion about departments and
provinces, however. This and the slip Linette
had made seemed to overshadow the earlier trouble
with Linette's stomach. She made a few faces
indicative of unsettled digestion as we rumbled
over great, muddy ruts in the road, but she was
definitely better.

A recent storm had raised the level of the brook
that crossed our road and just as we were looking
forward to our midday dinner, we found ourselves
stranded in the midst of a picturesque countryside
under a misty sky. The stop served several practical
purposes, but eventually we formed a line and made
our way across the bark-covered logs with a light
rain pelting our faces. It was not easy, while lifting
the robes of Sister Magdalen out of the mire. Linette
went skipping ahead because she heard her seven-

year-old enemy loudly boasting that he would go across hopping on one leg.

The child's mother, if indeed she was his mother, balanced herself immediately behind me and breathed noisily in my ear as she remarked, 'What a very curious mistake that guard at the barrier made last night!'

'How so?' I hoped my indifference would influence her.

'But Sister, your name of course. The lad calls you Magdalen Clare, yet my ears must have deceived me. Surely the guard referred to you on your passport papers as Sister Magdalen Marie.'

I stopped on the log, almost oversetting the woman. In my frostiest voice I said, 'You are quite correct, Citizeness.'

A large and unbecoming wrinkle appeared between her narrow brows.

'How so, Sister?'

'In that your ears deceived you.' I moved on, step by step. I was meanly pleased to hear a splash behind me, and to know the woman's foot had slipped into the icy stream. But my nun's habit required me to behave with a trifle more charity, so I turned and offered her my hand. As I brought her up close to me again, she peered directly into my face. It took all my strength to keep from betraying uneasiness at that scrutiny. Even so, she must have seen the flash of most unchristian anger in my eyes.

'But Sister, I am persuaded I heard the name Magdalen Marie last night.'

'Magdalen Marie Clare Pelletier. Are you quite satisfied, Citizeness?'

We had reached the shore and I walked up the wet, slippery bank, remembering to stride in the fashion of a true Sister Magdalen. I met the coach on the far side of the little hill. The passengers from the carriage roof were scrambling up on the imperial, but I saw nothing of Linette. She was undoubtedly inside the coach. I went rapidly across the field toward the coach, which had been driven around the hill along the muddy ruts of the road. I reached it after the Breton pair and the two Low-landers had climbed in and taken their seats.

Linette was not in the coach.

I stepped down again and went around to the far side of the coach, but the road fell off sharply here to the stream below and there was no sign of Linette or any other human being among the dun-coloured rushes that lined the stream. I retraced my steps to the low, rolling hill. Passengers were still straggling down to the coach. I hurried up among them and turned completely around, getting a view of the near countryside through the rain.

In spite of all my blundering efforts, the child put in my charge had vanished.

CHAPTER NINE

DURING my first minute of realisation, I felt numb with terror at the awful possibilities. I kept insisting madly to myself, it's a nightmare! It is not real. It is a hideous dream. I will wake in the coach and find the child beside me.

But I was not asleep. I had left the coach and followed – no – started to follow Linette across the log while the coach and the team took the old bridge. I had the stupid discussion with the woman about Sister Magdalen's correct name. Or was it such a stupid encounter, after all? Had it been a deliberate effort to distract my attention?

I should have known from the first; I had always suspected the woman and her obnoxious boy, and yet they had fooled me completely. I ran down to the coachman who was counting his passengers. He must have thought me an odd sight, my many robes slapping damply against my ankles, my coif soaked. I was far from the serene Sister Magdalen I had appeared to be. In my panic I clutched at the muscular, knotted arm of the coachman as he was in the act of twirling his ludicrous moustache. He was plainly in terror of my familiarity.

'Citizen! The young – boy I was escorting is gone. I can't find him anywhere.'

'What? The lad gone? Playing you a joke, most likely. But you'd best locate him, Sister. We'll be on our way in no time. We've a good many villages to

127

cover this day, and dinner next post. Can't be late for that.'

I was in such a panic that I wrung my hands as I pleaded, like a bad actor at the Theatre Feydau.

'Please tell me, are all your passengers accounted for? Perhaps one of them made off with my charge.'

With a sigh for his own patience he looked up at the imperial, then into the coach whose door stood open.

'The good Citizeness Bosquet and her son, Henri-Jacques, have not yet arrived. Ah! But they approach. That should be the whole of the seats booked from Paris, according to my waybill.'

The postilion had been at the head of the team and he came back to hear our conversation. I could not be troubled with him at the moment. I was anxious to see what the woman and child would say. Perhaps a confederate of theirs had made off with Linette while they kept me occupied.

I took a few strides, splashing mud over the hem of my robe as I did so, and I barred the way of the 'Citizeness Bosquet,' if, indeed, she was a mother and that obnoxious child was actually her property!

'Citizeness,' I began, trying not to show my suspicion or my deep fears. 'Your son and my charge were having a little game of it as we crossed the river back over the hill. Your son, therefore, must have seen the direction taken by young Citizen Léon Trouville, my charge.'

'My son saw nothing, Sister.' She shook the boy who had come up and was clinging to her middle. He looked up at me with those eyes which seemed so very wise that they were frightening, although there was no question that the boy was exactly what he appeared, a seven-year-old, badly reared child. He looked at the woman who called herself his mother. He nodded. If ever I had seen a boy prompted to an answer, it was this one. Swallowing my revulsion,

128

I tried to find him a charming and attractive child.

I said in the saintliest voice I could muster, 'What a very observant young man! But you must have seen the boy who was with me. You and he were at some game or other when we crossed the logs over the river.'

He shook his head, sealed his rubbery lips and looked up at the Citizeness Bosquet.

'I want to sit on top.'

'Ah well, you cannot. Come with me.' She held out her hand and he fastened onto it, but with his teeth. The woman boxed his ears and at the coach door he held back. 'I want to sit on top.'

I approached stealthily behind him. The Bosquet woman was about to refuse again but the coachman came to the boy's rescue.

'Plenty of room, Citizeness, and the good fellows will set him between them.'

The good fellows already up on the imperial didn't look in the least likely to enjoy his presence, but the woman said, 'Oh, very well! But only until the next post.' She got into the coach.

Behind the boy, I changed my tactics entirely and with every evidence of scorn, I remarked, 'You couldn't possibly see what happened. You are an infant. How could you see?'

He swung around, red-faced with indignation.

'I could! I saw them go. I'm not an infant.'

My heartbeat quickened, I am sure, but I laughed. 'How silly! Everyone knows no one is missing but Léon.'

'From the top of the coach! A man from the top of the coach. I did see them! I did!'

The Bosquet woman rapped smartly on the coach window and the boy subsided. I caught my breath. As the coachman swung the boy onto the imperial, where none too eager male hands caught him, I called after him, 'You couldn't possibly see which way he went. Not possibly!'

'I could. I could!' The boy leaned over a passenger's arm to yell, 'There! They went there!' He pointed to the east across the wide fields, the low-lying ponds and rushes, all appearing to float in the misty air. 'A man from up here. He went too.'

The coachman looked up at the passengers on the rooftop. They had been passing around a flask of cheap wine and paid little attention to him or the boy thrown into their midst.

'Ay!' the coachman said to me finally. 'Your lad seems to have run away from you with one of the passengers up there. We seem to be missing one, after all. Well!' His shrug was all too eloquent. 'We must go now. My belly tells me dinner is late.'

'But you must help me! You cannot leave two of your passengers here, wandering across the countryside. Who was that man from the roof?'

But by this time everyone had begun to peer down at me, curious to know what the delay might be. Had we not been so close to dinnertime, I am persuaded I would have received more assistance. As I glanced over each man, I discovered the missing face was that of the meek young man with nervous hands, the fellow who had seemed frightened by the quarrels between Linette and the obnoxious boy. Not so frightened now, I thought, trying to cover my fears with anger.

The postilion had mounted and was impatiently watching the coachman. One of the Breton men opened the door and waved his arms at us.

'On! Get on! We are late for the next post. We are starving, all of us!'

The coachman tried to push me up the steps. I flung his hand off, started across the muddy road to the field and into a sheet of rain. There was only one possible direction in which the man could have disappeared with Linette. At the far end of the field, dotted with marshy pools that reflected the sky, there was a seemingly endless row of poplars. They formed a black barrier and could provide a place of concealment. By the time I had realised Linette was gone, it seemed clear that she and her captor were behind that windbreak which had once served to mark the border of some nobleman's estate.

I tried once more to win the reluctant help of the coachman.

'Which direction does the coach road take when it curves around these fields?'

He pointed. It seemed to me that by following the coach road in its semicircle around the field, I would be brought much closer to the line of poplars and whatever lay behind it; for the road appeared to reach the poplars and then move southward almost parallel to them and to the meandering river. I got into the coach, to everyone's relief, and almost before the door was closed, the coach leaped forward and I fell into the lap of the stout Lowland lady who was not in the least polite about it. I shifted to my seat and sat there leaning forward, peering out the window, with my fingers tightly interlaced. I must have looked quite mad to the other passengers, but I had never known such dread, not even during the Terror.

Someone had taken Linette. It could not have been her father or one of his agents. I was certain he would never play me such a cruel trick. No, the brain behind this business was the principessa's, and for some unknown reason, she did not plan to kill Linette. She would scarcely have hired anyone to take the girl from me, when she could be poisoned so much more easily. Was there some other enemy?

Uncle Bernardo! The mysterious demon conjured up by the principessa. But was he a genuine demon, or simply one of the princess' fanciful ones? Marius did not fear him, or mention him as a possible danger. But Linette was gone. I scarcely knew what to think.

I stared out of the window until the semicircular highway crossed the line of poplars and moved south and east with the trees. The stream widened below, evidently preparatory to emptying into the Yonne River, which watered these regions. I now had a good view of the area behind the poplar grove and could see the only habitation, the burned-out remains of a half-timbered manor house and some outbuildings nearby. It was obviously still in use; a plume of smoke spiralled upward from the kitchen area across a shattered archway, part of the skeleton of the great house.

A narrow estate trail, doubtless deep in mud, wound its way to the group of buildings. Suddenly, as I watched behind our coach, I could see an ancient tumbrel, driven by a bent old man, plodding along the estate trail to join our highway. Someone in that building must have seen Linette and her captor. They must have gone directly across the property, since there was no other way they could have taken without being seen.

Now came the tumbrel loaded with winter vegetables. Turnips, I guessed, as the old nag in the shafts moved onto the road and behind us. The nag was not so old, after all. It seemed to make surprising speed. Peasants in a ruined farmhouse used such an excellent horse to pull a broken-down tumbrel of turnips? It was possible.

The tumbrel and the high stepping horse moved close behind the coach now. The top-heavy coach itself had begun to sway from side to side and I did not envy the passengers on the roof. The afternoon sun cast darts of light through the mist and it was not long before the rain had moved eastward, giving the fields a sparkling spring look. On the east side, the coach and its rooftop riders cast weird, elongated shadows across the muddy road and the slight elevation of the fields beyond. To the west, the poplars still accompanied us, casting their own lean shadows, like enormous fingers pointing to us.

The Breton on the east side of the coach exclaimed suddenly, 'The devil he is! That peasant means to catch us up.'

'To pass us, belike,' said his comrade. 'Next toll he means to beat us through.'

The Bosquet woman roused herself.

'No toll here since the Revolution. Through this part of the Department of the Yonne there is no more grinding a few sous from the starving poor. Ah! That child! He will kill himself yet!'

We all looked at the fascinating shadows playing across the eastern half of the road and pastures beyond. There was no mistaking the shadows of the obnoxious boy, wrestling with two of the men on the rooftop, as he tried to peer over at the horse and tumbrel which were rapidly coming alongside the coach. I was intending every minute to get down from the coach and look for Linette among the ruins of the manor house, when I discovered on closer inspection that the driver of the tumbrel, like his horse, was not what he appeared. As his cart and horse rattled along the road, the old peasant's storm cape and black bicorne hat did not conceal his face. It was a very nondescript face, easily forgotten, but I became convinced that this was the timid young man with nervous hands, who had made off with Linette.

The sleek, well-kept mare moved up rapidly beside the coach.

'A race! A race!' one of the Bretons cried, and both men pushed to that side of the coach to watch the fun. On my side of the carriage the Lowlander leaned across my body and in heavily accented

French offered a wager with the Bretons as he struck his fists against the window.

'The wagon wins. You will see.'

I was trying to thrust between these eager gamblers, to get a better look at the tumbrel and its cargo of turnips. If, of course, they *were* turnips, below that first layer. I could see the shadows struggling on the rooftop, trying to keep that impossible seven-year-old child from tumbling over into the tumbrel in his excitement.

By this time, however, our coachman was equally inspired. We picked up speed and went rattling and swaying along with the tumbrel and horse keeping pace beside us. Then the flying mane moved ahead gradually, past the coach door, now parallel to the coachman on his box. I was sure Linette was somewhere in that tumbrel, under all those turnips. I could only pray that she was still alive.

The road began to descend, and to narrow. I caught a glimpse of a riverbed again, with a dribble of water, but this was a welcome obstacle. Only one vehicle could cross the rocky bed at a time. Everything depended upon the coach reaching that other side first. From what we could see, it looked like a much narrower road beyond the riverbed.

'Village ahead,' called Breton.

Everyone loudly expressed his gratitude.

'Dinner at last,' said the Lowland lady as she finished her cheese.

It looked as though the tumbrel would reach the ford before us. I had been so frantic since discovering Linette's disappearance that this latest terrible possibility left me almost numb. The bets were raised. The Lowlander was now certain of his man. The Bretons still clung to the Lyon Coach.

But none of us counted on the dogged pride of the coachman and our young postilion. We tore along at a speed that felt like flying, missing half the rocks and boulders in the road. We rocked so badly that we threatened to overturn at any instant.

For my own reasons, I was cheering silently for our coach. It was the only way I could get back to that tumbrel. The driver would have to stop on the shore while our coach and team rattled and rumbled over the riverbed. But the tumbrel was opposite our coach door now, and moving forward. My knuckles pushed against the window. The men on either side of me were so excited over the outcome of what they conceived to be a simple race that they ignored my excitement.

Then, as we all held on, some praying, some cursing, our coachman and the postilion ahead of him began to cut our team over into the path of the speeding mare, and the driver of the tumbrel was forced to pull up short. Turnips rolled down off the mound in the centre of the tumbrel and I thought I caught a glimpse of something underneath. A long box.

Dear God! If there was a God, I prayed, 'Please do not let her be dead in that box!'

Our coach had moved forward so that the tumbrel again appeared opposite the coach door, and the long shadows of afternoon were once more cast across the tumbrel and its contents. The coach and team had pulled up at the river ford and the tumbrel, crowded against the pasture lining the east side of the highway, came to a halt as well, unable to pass the barrier of the coach's team. I was preparing to get the door open, to spring out and demand that he uncover the box, when the commotion from the rooftop caught everyone's attention.

The Bosquet woman's boy had been so enthused over the race that he slipped out of the hands of those passengers trying to save him and tumbled over the side. His mother and I screamed. The boy plunged outward, seemed to twist around like a cat in midair,

135

and landed on his feet, sunk in the turnips in the middle of the tumbrel.

He was too dazed by his experience to answer the cries of everyone in the coach as the door was flung open and the steps let down. I piled out with the others, the boy's mother running around to the back of the tumbrel where one of the Bretons released some slats and the boy ploughed through the turnips until he half-jumped and was half-carried down in the arms of the Breton. His mother squeezed him hard, then scolded him in shrill tones, and yanking his arm, dragged him to the coach.

Meanwhile, I was crying to anyone who would listen, 'Please examine the tumbrel. The box. Examine the box beneath the turnips. That is the man who snatched up Miss – Master Léon!'

The coachman and the postilion were busy leading team and coach across the ford and the driver of the tumbrel did not look around. I pointed this out to the obliging Breton.

'Don't you see? He is the passenger who deserted the coach back there by the river crossing. Make him show his face. He has stolen the young boy I was delivering to his parents.'

Perhaps the dark Breton was moved by my nun's habit. Brittany had remained Catholic long after the practice of religion went out of fashion in Paris. At all events, he behaved in the most obliging way at these frantic accusations of mine. While I was begging him to examine the long box, so like a coffin, that had been uncovered in the child's scramble to get out, he strode along to the driver of the tumbrel.

'Come down, Monsieur,' the Breton commanded, using the old-fashioned mode of address.

The man in the bicorne hat shrugged as though he did not understand. He was pretending to be a simple peasant of the province, but the Breton called sternly, 'No play-acting, rogue! Those hands of yours are no peasant's hands.'

The supposed peasant looked down at his fingers tangled in the reins. He was excessively nervous. The Breton's comrade, hearing this odd conversation, came up to reinforce his friend, and the result was that the fellow got up from the straw coachman's box, dropped to the ground with a readiness that stunned me, and agreed to uncover the box.

Everyone climbed down from the rooftop of the coach and crowded around the back of the tumbrel. The driver of the tumbrel stepped carefully among the turnips. He kicked away the turnips and slipped off the cover of the box. We all stood on our toes and tried to look inside the box. The man reached in, drew up a scythe and a long bundle of broomstraws.

There was a silence of stupefaction that broke into laughter. Everyone stared at me. I felt ready to sink, not from embarrassment but from panic and fury, for I was convinced this man knew where Linette was.

Someone helped me up the steps into the coach, as I protested every step of the way. I heard men behind me making apologies to the man with nervous hands, who climbed back on the woven basket covered by a board which he used as a seat, and took up the reins. I heard what seemed to be a dozen voices explaining to the nervous man and to each other that Sisters of Mercy sometimes went a bit over the border because of their very solitary life, came to imagine the devil was in all things.

By the time everyone was back in his place within the coach we were already crossing the ford. Most of the passengers complained loudly about the mud, the tangled rushes and the size of the stones in the creek bottom, but I found myself with a roaring headache while I tried to understand how the fellow had made away with Linette. She must have been left at the ruined manor houses, perhaps in the custody of those people responsible for the smoke I had seen rising from some hearth within the out-buildings of the estate.

He could not have murdered Linette! Over and over, I repeated this in my thoughts, hoping to believe it. But I was convinced by this time that as soon as we reached the next village, I must hire a horse and cart and return to that not-quite-forsaken manor house.

We soon made out the spire of the local church half a league further along and great sighs went up from my fellow passengers.

'The next post. Name of God! It is time,' one of the Bretons exclaimed. 'I have never known such hunger.'

Even I roused myself, determined to find someone in the village who would take me back to that manor house. A soldier, perhaps. I knew that one of General Bonaparte's men would help me if I explained how the daughter of one of his officers had been abducted. But underneath every thought, every plan, was the dreadful possibility that Linette was already dead, that she had been murdered. I crushed my fists into my eyes. 'I will not think of that!'

As the coach and horses rattled into the neat, rain-washed Burgundian village and headed toward what appeared to be the only inn, I sat up stiffly, ready to throw myself out of the carriage and run for help. Behind us, all too close, was the tumbrel and horse of the man I suspected.

Somewhat to the surprise of the grinning postilion who came to open the door and let down the steps, I pushed my way between the Bretons and the Lowlander and was the first out of the coach. But my heavy robes hampered me and it took an enormous effort to rush past the coach's box and the sweating team and into the inn, before the hungry passengers poured through behind me.

The innkeeper, a stout man with a bald spot that looked like a tonsure, met me with loquacious respect.

'Sister! Blessed Holy Mary! How good it is to see your habit! We've become heathens of late. But you are ill. The travel sickness, one understands all too well in these wretched coaches. Come. Take a seat in our private chamber. I'll send in some good, strengthening mulled wine. The very thing.'

I grasped at his fleshy hand that was moist and smelled of the mutton roasting on the spit in the public room across the hall. Several travellers were already seated around the fire with their booted feet upon the fender.

'If you please, Citizen, a man has made away with my charge, a young lad who vanished from the coach. The man is driving into town at this very minute.'

The Bosquet woman came in behind me with her son and the two Bretons. They were in time to see the innkeeper tearing off his stained apron while he promised me, 'Show me the fellow! I'll attend to him.'

'No, no! We've searched the tumbrel. I believe he left her at a house a league from here. But he must tell . . .'

There was an absolutely deafening chorus behind me as the passengers demanded their dinner and the Citizeness Bosquet explained as she got in the innkeeper's way, 'Our dinner first, if you please. We all searched the young man's tumbrel. He was not in the least hesitant. He had nothing to hide. You see, the good sister is greatly troubled,' and she had the audacity to tap her bonnet above the ear significantly. Before I could counter this lie, the Bretons and even several passengers from the rooftop of the coach joined the woman in her opinion

139

of me, nodding and pointing to their skulls, insinuating that I was mad.

The poor innkeeper could not but be persuaded. He looked from one to the other of them, while I was trying to put in another plea. 'I know the fellow cannot have taken the child with him. The tumbrel was searched as they say, but I wish to take a horse and a cart and drive back to the manor house where he obtained the tumbrel.' I could see the growing doubt in his face as everything I said proved my companions were right about me. Then too, one glance would have told him that I, like the thin-faced, nervous man outside, had never handled reins in my life. How I would handle a cart and horse, I hadn't the least notion, but I would manage.

The innkeeper's round, friendly face sagged. 'Good Sister, this is a post for the Lyon Coach. These people must dine. They are late now. Perhaps later we may . . . yes. Later.'

I swung around, hearing familiar sounds in the street.

'You don't understand. The criminal himself could tell you what he had done. He could be made to tell you. He is driving up now. Do not water his horse, or help him. Make him wait. I implore you!'

I might as well have pleaded with the elements. I had lost my battle against the conviction of my fellow passengers that my wits were addled and I only imagined my runaway ward was in danger. I heard the scraping of a chair near the fireplace in the big public room as it was pushed back and someone arose, but I was much too interested in my own problems to glance in that direction. I turned and rushed out to the street to find another stable in this benighted town.

As I hurried into the road I was nearly run down by the young man with the nervous hands. The fleet-footed mare did not quite tread on me, but I only just caught myself before falling flat in the mud under the horse's hooves. I waved a fist at the young man who stood up and lashed out at the mare as if he would try to set the animal on me.

'Have a care, Sister,' the fellow called, and in that horrifying moment I knew he did intend to run me down.

I shook my fist again in a manner not very Christian, screaming, 'What have you done with her? Abductor! Traitor! Aristo!' I was hoping at least one of my accusations would win me support among the villagers.

I won that support in a most astonishing quarter. Behind me a voice that would have delighted me in normal circumstances terrified me in this situation where I had so lamentably betrayed his trust.

Marius Redon's voice demanded, 'Answer the sister!'

Beside my mud-crusted deep sleeve, I saw Captain Redon's thin, steady hand reach for the harness on the mare. I gasped, sure he would be crushed, but under his hand the mare quieted to a trembling stillness in spite of the screamed commands of the driver.

CHAPTER TEN

'AND now,' Marius said calmly, 'what is this all about? You in the tumbrel, why did you wish to run down the good sister?'

Not knowing what to do, I took great care to follow Captain Redon's lead. For the moment I did nothing.

'N-no,' the nervous man insisted. 'Ask them. Anyone. I've done no harm. You may search the tumbrel. Nothing. Only farm tools and turnips.'

Marius glanced at me. I nodded. I thought Marius himself was concealing his tension very well, but it was there all the same. He soothed the skittish mare while I explained briefly, 'This man was a passenger up on the imperial of the coach. He disappeared at the same time that Lin—Léon disappeared.'

All the while, as our fellow passengers began to gather in the doorway of the inn, Marius was studying the man seated precariously on a board over the big woven basket that served as a driver's seat. The fellow was peering down at us in terror.

Staring at him and the rig itself, Marius said to me, 'He is much too frightened. Léon must be somewhere about. Otherwise, he would have simply mounted the horse and galloped off instead of taking along this tumbrel.'

I hadn't reasoned this way, but my hopes began to revive. If Linette was dead, he would have buried her, would he not?

'But we examined the tumbrel,' I told him again.

'Then Léon is not in the tumbrel. And what does that leave us?'

Even I could see that this question sent the nervous man into a frenzy. He stood up and made as if to jump down.

'Remove the board you are sitting on,' Marius ordered him in a quiet voice that could still be heard by all the fascinated witnesses in the muddy street and the inn doorway.

Shaking badly, the fellow obeyed. I looked quickly at Marius. I fancied his mouth was almost colourless with the effort required to retain that calm, but he suddenly left the horse and swung himself up lightly beside the driver, thrusting him away. Then he unfastened the basket seat and raised the lid.

We all held our breaths with suspense. No one moved. He reached in and lifted out what appeared to be the cramped and lifeless body of Linette Redon. A hiss of shock and dismay rose from all those watching. He touched his cheek to hers as he held her. I could not guess what he had discovered until, a few seconds later, she began to squirm in his arms.

A ripple of relieved comment and gentle laughter spread through the crowd. I think only I heard Linette's first words, 'Oh, Marius, I thought I was done for!'

He turned to me, and slipped her down. I caught her while she slid through my arms but could not stand on her own feet for a few minutes.

'My legs are asleep,' she apologised, and I held her securely while she tested first one foot on the ground and then the other.

Marius dropped down beside us. His hand was curled into a fist and the knuckle of his thumb pressed hard against his breastbone, although he talked rapidly to keep us from noticing that he was in pain.

'Well, Léon, you must have squirmed about in that basket. I was sure I saw it move.'

Linette giggled. 'I did. I called out. I yelled. But it was all muffled. He wrapped a sheet around me and I have a dreadful headache. He made me swallow some vile drink.'

'Come,' I suggested, remembering what these exertions must have cost Marius. 'We'll go in and sit by the fire. Your hands are freezing.'

'Oh, but I am perfectly—' Marius had thrown his travel cloak around her and she read something in my eyes. She went on in a neat change of track, ' – I am perfectly delighted to sit by a fire after all that bumping up and down.'

With a pretence that the rest was entirely for our rescued heroine, Linette and I persuaded Marius to come with us into the private parlour of the inn where a smaller fire burned somewhat smokily in the grate. He had been about to go after the abductor, but that luckless individual was running through the village in a rain of mud and stones hurled at him by the indignant crowd that had witnessed Linette's rescue. Some of them threw sticks to trip up the fellow. I knew Marius would want to question him but from the stiff tightness of his face and the dark smudges under his eyes, I thought we would be fortunate to get him to that comforting fire.

As we entered the private parlour, I held back a moment and spoke with the sympathetic innkeeper. 'Can you bring us some hot mulled wine as you suggested?'

'Just so, Sister. Just so. And there's good bread left from the night's baking. Not too stale yet.'

Marius had started to sit on the hearth but Linette had persuaded him to take one of the two cushioned chairs and to put his booted feet up on the warm

145

fender while she knelt beside him, leaning against his knee and rubbing her feet absently. She had removed her boots, and I saw at once that they were set much too close to the fire. I came in as quietly as possible, not wanting to disturb the father and daughter as she breathlessly related her adventure to him.

I set her boots a trifle further away from the flames so they would not curl up and dry improperly, and then sat in the other chair and put my hands out to warm them at the fire.

Marius leaned forward as Linette was still happily chattering away about what she called her 'thrilling doings.' He took the fingers of her right hand between his hands and she, apparently understanding this signal to be silent, stopped speaking on the instant and looked over her shoulder. He assured her gently, 'No, no, chérie. There is no danger. But I must go after that rogue and question him.'

The jolly innkeeper had arrived with a heavy tray covered by a napkin, and heard this.

'Not so, Monsieur. That is to say – Citizen. Our good folk have the child's abductor. He's a bit the worse for it, but he deserves a cuffing and more.'

Marius had started for the door. I did not dare to interfere but Linette exchanged a quick, worried glance with me and said, 'Please, Father, let them keep him for awhile. I'm much colder than I thought, and I don't want to be left alone. Maybe the old harridan has other agents waiting for me . . . if you please?'

'Where is he?' Marius demanded of the innkeeper. He had started up but Linette kept her hold upon one of his hands.

The innkeeper set the tray on the hob by the fire. 'In my turnip cellar. Was that well done of me?'

We all burst into laughter. 'Exactly where he

146

deserves to be,' Linette said, summing up all our feelings.

Marius allowed himself to be pulled back to his chair by Linette, while I poured a big pewter cup full of steaming spiced wine. He must have been feeling in some pain because he took the cup without protest and began to drink. Over the lip of the cup his dark eyes thanked me without words. I poured water into Linette's cup, weakening the potency of the wine, and broke off some of the bread which she chewed ravenously.

Drinking my own wine, I said finally, 'You were not surprised to find your father here, were you, Linette?'

'Oh, but I was! He intended to meet us at Joigny. That's a later post stop. I daresay you wondered why I went off with that perfect great silly, the Turnip Man, but he told me he had a pistol in the pocket of his greatcoat. I didn't see how he could. It was a very small pocket. But I looked and it really was a pistol, a little one. So I went. I thought I might push him away and run, but I never had the chance. He made me run across that field and when we reached the farm next to the great house, he made me swallow some drops in water. Ugh!'

'Laudanum!' I exclaimed.

Linette added with a certain pride, 'He was supposed to sell me into slavery in the Ottoman Empire. Through Marseilles, I think. Isn't that exciting?'

Marius smiled at her attitude and tickled her neck, but I was horrified.

'Can they do such a monstrous thing?'

'Of course they can!' Linette said. 'It happens every day. But I didn't think I was pretty enough. Actually, it was better than killing me, which I daresay they had rather do.'

'I doubt that being sold into some Kurdistan

147

camel driver's harem is better than death,' I said.

But it was clear that I wasn't going to convince Linette, although Marius looked over her head at me, understanding my horror quite well. To take his daughter's mind off the exciting fate she had escaped, he explained to me, 'I assure you, Clare, I made my plans to meet the coach on the road, not because I mistrusted you, but because I – because—'

I looked at him and smiled. For the first time in our acquaintance, I had confused him.

'I understand perfectly. It was clever of you. Did you also continue to pretend you were dying?'

'Sister Magdalen had a splendid burial service planned for me, but we decided our tactics might be a trifle obvious, especially as I was gaining in strength all the while; so I bribed my way into the mail coach and arrived here two hours before you.'

'But Father, you were to meet us at Joigny!'

He hesitated. I guessed from the tired way he answered her that he had been unable to go further and had been forced to stop at this little village from sheer physical exhaustion, but he made up some tale of having heard the wine was excellent here. 'And it is excellent, is it not?'

'It's sour!' Linette contradicted him with a wrinkled nose. 'Father, are you feeling quite the thing?'

He laughed at her use of one of those cant expressions brought back to Paris by the military after contacts with the English in such international marketplaces of espionage as the Venetian Republic. He repeated with emphasis, 'I am feeling quite the thing. Don't I look it?'

'You look wonderful. I was never so glad to see anyone.'

'I daresay you were. There was certainly nothing to look at in that basket in which I found you.'

Henceforth, Linette and I avoided the subject of

148

her father's illness and the atmosphere was much happier. But we were infinitely relieved when he postponed questioning the man in the turnip cellar until after he had eaten a very late dinner with us. It was well into the evening when he and the inn-keeper went down into what appeared to be the bowels of the earth to question the prisoner.

The Lyon Coach had long since left us behind, and Linette and I discovered during our long, anxious wait for Marius that the inn would be hard put to accommodate us overnight.

'One chamber only, I regret. But it is so,' the innkeeper's wife explained. 'The gentleman must sleep in a chair in the private parlour.'

We didn't like it, but in the end we had to agree, until Marius returned with news that changed our plans. He was either working on sheer nerve and determination, or he thrived on hazards. He came striding to us in the private parlour with his travel cape flung over one shoulder.

'We must be on our way. We've no time to lose.' To his daughter, he added, 'Chérie, the innkeeper's boy has obligingly sold me a cloak for you. It may be too long. Let us see.'

He placed the brown material around her shoulders and Linette, with an eye to drama, threw the right end of the cloak over her left shoulder and made a fine classic figure while we applauded her. I half expected Marius to be quick-tempered and impatient with his daughter's playfulness at such a moment, like any busy father, but he was surprisingly gentle with her.

How he managed to secure in that tiny village a gig and a mare of mature but not senile years, I could not understand, until we were on the point of departure and the innkeeper's wife confessed to me, 'I should not, perhaps, say this, especially to you, Sister, but the gentleman is very persuasive, very charming. So much so that I felt – that is, my husband felt, you should be warned. Not that a gracious and saintly person like yourself would be tempted, but . . . How far do you travel in his company, Sister?'

I laughed and assured her, 'I believe I am aware of the gentleman's persuasive ways. And being aware, I am protected.'

'Good. One never knows, these benighted days, when priests and nuns deny their God and behave as one hears they behave in Paris. Will you pray for me, Sister? We have our church, but it was desecrated in '94 and we have not had a priest since. Sister, your blessing?'

Marius and Linette looked back to find out what was detaining me and saw me just as the good woman touched my rosary and crucifix to her lips. I felt guilty at my hypocrisy and scurried away to join them. At least during this stop I had been able to remove the gown beneath my habit and was carrying it in a small valise. I could scarcely wait for the time when I would be given permission to change into that gown and become myself once more. Living up to the high ideals of the woman who had worn this habit was proving to be hard on my conscience.

We crossed into the little gig, while I thought it must look a trifle peculiar for a nun to dash across the landscape in the company of a pair of handsome males, even though one of them was only twelve! Once we were on our way, with Marius handling the reins, Linette and I tried not to worry about him. He seemed to know what he was doing but we had a ride of more than two hours and could only hope for the best.

At least there would be a decent bed for him in the large post town of Joigny. Linette and I were in a silent conspiracy to preserve the health of her father. He, on his side, had his own secrets which he would not confide to us. I was certain there was still danger, else why were we hurrying through the night in this haphazard fashion? We were certainly many days from the Lombardy Plain, which was our goal.

I broke the uneasy silence as we rode through the deep, starless night.

'Captain Redon, what is to become of that man who abducted Linette? And did he know then that she was a girl? He must have, or why else would he have intended to sell her into Barbary?'

Linette shook her head. 'He kept calling me "lad" and "boy" and saying one day I would thank him.'

Marius and I exchanged looks. Mine, I know, was full of horror and his was grim enough to tell me he had known this bit of news through his questioning of the fellow.

'Will he be tried at Joigny?' I asked. 'Or at Lyon?'

'Neither, since we will not be present to testify. He will be held for a week or so, until his leg heals. Some careless villager cracked his thigh with a well-placed stone. After that, it will depend upon the villagers.' He peered ahead along the dark road. Only a single lamp suspended from the side of the gig cast any illumination upon the muddy ruts that served as our highway.

'But what if the fellow should escape and come after us?' I asked anxiously.

He smiled a cold, rather frightening smile. 'We aren't running from that rogue, but in order to reach Lyon in time to catch the Alpine Coach. It leaves on Christmas night.'

'How odd,' Linette murmured, 'that it must be Christmas night!'

'Only because we are likely to run into impossible weather during these winter months, and the coach

151

takes advantage of any period of fair weather. If we don't leave with the Christmas coach, a storm may prevent us from crossing the Mont Cenis Pass.'

'Captain,' I said, when I had considered this fresh danger. 'You haven't told us whether Linette's abductor was hired by the principessa.'

Linette and I looked at him. After a momentary hesitation, he surprised us both. 'The fellow has nothing to do with her. He was simply an enterprising young rogue, apparently of good family, who had found a way to make a little money. I daresay, he might have persuaded other victims without having to resort to pistols and laudanum.'

I laid out the real matter then as calmly as I could. 'In plain language, we have yet to meet the principessa's men.'

'In plain words, yes.'

I felt Linette shiver between us and Marius must have felt this, too, for he looked at her and cheered her immediately by his joking reassurance, 'Come now. You'll not tell me you are frightened when you have both a soldier and a Holy Sister to defend you?'

'But of course not!' she scoffed, and made a valiant attempt to show us she was as bold as anyone. I squeezed her hand briefly in what I hoped was a gesture of comfort, and she made the odd and infinitely touching remark, 'I am really the luckiest girl in the Hôtel Dieu to have you both to help me.'

Marius said nothing to this and seemed to be concentrating on the road. I wondered if he was so busy thinking about dangers to come that he had not even heard her curious remark. As for his attitude to me, it was quite evident he did not completely trust me, and what feelings he did extend to me were those of an employer. It was a dreadful setback, and whatever my feelings toward him might be, I was well aware that they must be kept in close check. Nothing would drive him further from me than a fawning adoration without the slightest hint of reciprocity. And besides all else, he had many reasons for a lack of trust in me. Had I not lost Linette a second time?

We came again upon the sparkling Yonne River, and knew we must be nearing the hill town of Joigny. The river banks, lined with wintry little trees and rushes, could not destroy the beauty of the river itself, and the sight of it seemed to lift our spirits. Presently we saw ahead of us the climbing streets of the post town with its narrow, huddled, medieval houses, each severely darkened and closed to the dangerous world of the street.

Not a soul seemed abroad though we did see in the the distance what might be the night crier's lamp, but Marius seemed to know where we were going. Unfortunately, two inns were full, and we went on through the town and pulled up before a two-storey, half-timbered inn whose sign, lighted by a flickering storm lantern, announced it to be The Duchy, featuring a gaudily painted face of that fifteenth-century Burgundian who nearly overthrew the Kingdom of France.

While Linette and I huddled together, more for reasssurance than against the cold, Marius went in and arranged for our accommodation. It was not until he had ordered the last two available rooms, on the first floor above the innyard, that he realised his problem. He and his 'son' were expected to share one room, and the good sister whom they were apparently escorting to the post town of Arney le Duc on the road to Lyon, was naturally to have a room alone. The innkeeper's lean and narrow-eyed wife was adamant that 'the lad' should not share the nun's bed. An awkward business, all around.

'You are fortunate,' she assured us. 'If we had more patrons, they would, of necessity, share the parlour I am giving you citizens. It is a public parlour, when all is said.'

When Marius, both amused and exasperated, came out to explain all this, we decided to accept the terms and make our own arrangements later. There were a number of patrons in the taproom, all of them male, and they looked up with varying degrees of interest as we went through the central passage leading to the dark staircase.

'How it creaks underfoot!' Linette whispered to me excitedly. 'At least we can hear if anyone tries to come upon us in the night.'

Marius pinched her chin. 'Let us devoutly hope no one comes upon us in the night, whether he creaks, or otherwise.'

The rooms assigned to us were joined by a door which the innkeeper's wife assured me privately could be bolted from my side. The room in which we stood was a parlour with a settee that looked monumentally hard.

'The lad can sleep there,' the woman announced, 'and the gentleman on the chaise. Both are by the fire, you will note. You, Sister, will be comfortable in the bedchamber. It also opens upon the corridor, should you decide to visit our local church for early Mass.'

I thanked her as graciously as I could, although I was aware of Marius' amusement as he watched me. He then ordered a supper to be served in the parlour. As the woman was leaving, he called to her, 'And three large ewers of hot water.'

The woman looked so appalled at this request for water in the land of good wines, that I had to turn away to stifle my laughter. But Marius had understood all too well that we three, or at all events, I, had rather wash than eat. The water

154

arrived with the trays of food and of course, a pair of large carafes of red wine.

Linette and I retired to the dusty bedroom and removed most of our garments to wash. Linette was wildly happy to sleep in a bed with a real tester and I felt it tactless of me to carp over the fact that the bed curtains had obviously not been shaken, much less cleaned, in the last ten years. I was surprised that Linette was not used to canopied beds. Surely, as Marius Redon's daughter and the heiress to the fabulous Visconti fortune, she had slept in such beds during her babyhood.

I had removed my coif but retained Sister Magdalen's habit as we came out to join Marius at the heavy Jacobean table, and it was a joy to see Linette eat. I did not quite believe Marius though, when he claimed we were so long at our toilette that he had nearly finished his own meal. He had very little appetite and spent the hour drinking the wine instead. He showed few signs of drunkenness, and certainly appeared the better for it afterward, but I shuddered to think in what case I should be if I drank so much.

Linette and I did well by the poached fish and the roast of kid, proof of Burgundian culinary prowess. We pretended not to notice our companion's lack of appetite or the fact that he presently jerked off the white cravat at his throat as if it choked him. He sat there with us so naturally, and as I watched him without seeming to, I felt a warmth and passion and then desire within me that I had never believed I could feel for any human being. My fingers trembled, dropping my napkin, and I reached down to pick it up.

Unfortunately for my attempt at poise, Marius reached for my napkin at the same time and in returning it, brought my fingers to his lips and kissed them. I do not know who was more astonished, Linette or I. I sipped my wine with determined calm.

The devil in Marius made him watch me so that I had nowhere to look. Finally, he poured more wine for himself, and remarked, looking into the glass with a flicker of a smile, 'Thank God, it is only a borrowed habit, Sister Clare.'

Linette's eyebrows nearly came together as she tried to understand this exchange. As for me, I must have flushed scarlet, but the moment ended all too soon. Linette kicked my ankle under the table.

'I'm dreadfully tired, Clare. Should we go to sleep in that wonderful bed with curtains?'

I knew she was thinking of her father, and I made a pretence of yawning and we excused ourselves and made ready to leave him. Linette went over and curtseyed before her father. He kissed her on the forehead, wished her a good night, reminded her that we would be leaving early, and watched us go to the bedchamber door. Then he said to me in that faintly lazy voice which belied the dark seriousness of his eyes, 'Aren't you going to wish me good night, Sister Clare?'

I smiled and returned to the table. 'Good night, Citizen.'

'Properly.' But in spite of the command, the charade was lightly played.

I went down on one knee before his chair. He kissed my forehead.

'Now, that is a proper good night, Sister Clare.'

I looked into his eyes as I arose. My feelings were such that I could not speak, so I turned and went across the room and at last, in the doorway with Linette, I was able to repeat in a calm voice, 'Good night, Citizen.'

I closed the door slowly, shutting us away from

this man I was learning to love with a passion I had so often heard extolled, but never before felt in myself.

Linette explained to me gently, 'You mustn't mind if he teases you, Clare. It is his way. And he means no harm.'

'I shall try to remember that.'

She put her head on one side, thoughtfully regarding me. 'I wonder if – don't you think you had rather marry him than your old betrothed?'

'I hadn't thought about it.'

She added eagerly, 'You would be happier, I know. Marius is exactly your sort.'

I could not agree with her more, but I did not say so.

She began to take off her boots which, despite all our efforts, had managed to dry in a way that curled the leather. 'I'm not sleepy, you know. I only said that for his sake.'

'I understand.' She looked so brave and dishevelled in her boyish masquerade that I added, 'Would you like me to brush your hair?'

She thought it a capital idea and, as I had suspected, it also made her sleepy so that when we climbed up the steps into the big bed, I thought she would sleep at once. To my surprise she sat up, crossed herself, and said a little prayer. 'Holy Mother, please keep Marius well and don't let him suffer, and I vow a silver candlestick in the Duomo. Thank you.'

She began to curl up on her side of the great bed. My own thoughts were very like hers and I was startled out of them by her sudden, blunt question, 'Don't you pray, Clare?'

'No, dear.'

'Why not?'

'It would be hypocritical. We fought a revolution against privilege, the Church as well as the nobility.'

157

She thought about this. 'It's very odd.' Then she turned over and went to sleep.

As for me, if my thoughts were not prayers, they were very near, who then was the hypocrite? I asked myself before I dozed off.

It was also Linette who woke me some time deep in the night by falling out of bed. I turned over, reached for her in the dark, then, as she seemed to have landed without danger, I leaned over her side of the bed and inquired what was the matter.

'Sh! I heard someone on the stairs and then the floor outside Father's door.'

'Probably another guest of the inn. You had better come back to bed or you will take a cold.' But I might as well have been talking to the carpet. She was already tiptoeing to the door between our room and the outer parlour where Marius slept.

Surely, if anyone did try to get in, Marius would be the first to hear. Nevertheless, in my petticoat – for I had no nightgown to sleep in – I got up on my side of the bed and went around to the door between the rooms, feeling my way from the light between the portières which were not quite drawn together.

'Stay back,' I told her. 'I'll see to it.' She was fumbling around in the semidark and suddenly pushed into my hand a set of broomstraws attached to a long handle. Armed with this, I opened the door quietly and looked in. The fire burned brightly, evidence to me that Marius must have kept it going all night. He had drawn one end of the chaise nearer the fire and was bundled in his travelling cloak, but I thought he did not appear to be asleep.

Someone rapped on the corridor door and at the same time the latch was tried from the outside. There was no bolt on the door and it opened even as Marius, seeing me, motioned me back. I stood in the bedchamber doorway clad in nothing but my petticoat, armed with my long-handled broomstraws.

A very big man with a grenadier's moustache strode in with his cloak flying dramatically. One felt that he was aware of the effect. He was in the middle of the room before he saw Marius quietly regarding him, with one of his quizzical smiles.

By the firelight I saw the big intruder clearly, and for an instant or two felt faint. I knew this fellow very well. I had been betrothed to him for nearly six years, and was still his affianced wife. He seemed a good deal more theatrical, a little too big, too obvious, since I last saw him. But he was Paul Vallier.

'My excuses, Citizen,' he said politely, straining to get a good look at Marius in the firelight. 'The innkeeper told me I might ask to share this room with you and your son. I shall pay the full reckoning, of course. I insist upon that. The other parlours are quartering half a dozen travellers. The Christmas season, you know. And not another inn available, I am sure. I can roll up beside the fire. I shan't trouble you. I will be leaving early on my way to Paris, on a matter of business. And,' he added with a slight smirk, 'to see my betrothed.'

Something, some slight sound or other made him turn in my direction, to see me, his betrothed, in the doorway, complete with petticoat and long-handled broomstraws, my hair falling untidily down my almost naked back.

CHAPTER ELEVEN

BEFORE Paul could express what must have been both stupefaction and the beginnings of righteous fury, I surprised myself by greeting him with all the calm and ease at my command.

'Good evening, Paul! How pleasant that you could meet us so much sooner than you had intended, and what a coincidence, my dear!' For the benefit of Marius and Linette, I added, 'This gentleman was – is my betrothed, Paul Vallier, currently of Geneva. A protégé of the principessa, I believe.' That would put the Redons on their guard.

Marius opened his eyes a little wider, the only sign that he too had been caught unaware and hadn't guessed the identity of the big, intrusive traveller. But he was able to recover much more quickly than poor Paul. Marius followed my lead, with what a sensitive man in Paul's place would have found to be a maddening serenity.

'If he is fortunate enough to be your betrothed, Citizeness Dubeque, I should envy him, were I not a poor wreck of the man I once was. But come. Bed yourself before the fire, Citizen. I haven't the least objection in the world.'

Paul finally managed to get out a few indignant words as he approached me with gravity and deliberation.

'Clare! What does this mean? How can you appear in such a condition in the eyes of a stranger like this – er – gentleman? Even though he may be a wreck of – that is—' Having reached me, he seemed to forget his grievance briefly and embraced me under the interested gaze of Marius Redon.

'I am travelling with the gentleman and his child as a governess for the child, and a nurse for the gentleman.' I wished I had not said this latter, as nurses could scarcely recommend themselves to a very proper man like Paul Vallier; their reputation was only slightly higher than that of an opera dancer. Another idea occurred to me as well. If Paul gave us trouble, there was one threat we might hold over his head; he certainly could not be travelling through France with his own passport papers. He had deserted the army years ago and was probably a wanted man. I wasn't sure whether Marius intended that Paul should know his actual identity, so I went on, 'This gentleman was injured in battle, and is an invalid, you understand.'

Marius coughed dramatically and grinned at me behind Paul's back. When my betrothed swung around, Marius said between the most affecting coughs, 'Captain Redon, at your service,' and added delicately, 'I am delighted to make the acquaintance of Citizen Paul Vallier.'

There was only the faintest emphasis on his own military title in comparison with Paul's civilian status, and I daresay he threw in his little jab because he did not like to be thought a complete 'wreck.' But I was amused, and found myself astonishingly indifferent to Paul's suspicion of my moral status. I urged Linette forward and she bowed politely to Paul, who realised Linette must be a female, but as she bowed in boyish fashion, and had her hair cropped, he scarcely knew how to behave toward her.

He said severely, 'Clare, I should like to speak with you, in private, when you have made yourself decent.'

'Tomorrow, Paul,' I dismissed him impatiently. 'It is much too late. And please don't keep Captain Redon from his sleep, either. Good night, my dear.' I closed the door. Linette leaned against it for a few minutes, listening, then came to bed.

'It is all quiet now. Your big friend has rolled up in his cloak on the floor. I hope he doesn't snore and keep father awake.'

'I have a notion your father will let Paul know if that happens. Captain Redon seems eminently able to defend himself.'

But for me, this was not the problem. How far would Paul go if he thought we would expose him to the first army post we came to, not to mention the French border! I lay in the darkness long after Linette slept, wondering whether Paul had been sent by the principessa, or at least by his sister Sylvie, to watch over us. I still could not believe the Paul Vallier I had known and cared for for so many years was capable of betraying either Marius or Linette to a hired cutthroat, as I was sure the principessa intended. Paul said he had come upon us accidentally on his way to meet me. But unquestionably, he had been shocked to see us together. I wondered if I would have a bad time of it on the morrow. But curiously enough, Paul's opinion of my morals no longer troubled me so greatly. I had learned this on the instant I realised what our appearance might have indicated to him tonight.

I was just going to sleep at last when I thought, 'Now he will know Marius is not back in Paris at the Hôtel Dieu. He may try and send a message to Paris, or to the principessa's agents along the way, wherever he – or they – might be. I must remember to warn Linette. We could never permit Paul to go off alone. Either Linette or I, or Marius, must be with him at all times.' His arrival was a maddening and potentially dangerous development. To me, this in itself was a remarkable discovery, for I had been willing, even eager, to marry Paul Vallier for almost six years.

I wondered to what use we could put the threat of exposure, for I supposed his passport papers would get him arrested at any time we chose to tell the truth about his identity. Could we use this as a kind of hint, a bribe not quite expressed in words, to keep him from betraying us? I went to sleep still planning Machiavellian schemes.

I was awakened by highly congenial voices in the next room and discovered that Linette had probably joined the socialising of Marius and Paul. I don't know why I should have found this annoying but I did. Wondering what the hour might be, I got out of bed and drew the window draperies apart. There was good transparent glass in the long windows, from which I assumed the inn must be the best in the town. Paul always chose the best, if possible. The equalising processes of the Revolution had never really appealed to him. He had, however, made a serious miscalculation in deserting the French army only months before its fantastic successes under General Bonaparte.

It now began to appear that Paul's arrival at this inn actually was a coincidence. I hoped, partly for his sake and partly for ours, that he had not sold himself to the principessa. He had never seemed as weak as Sylvie, or succumbed as easily to various temptations.

I sighed, crossed my fingers, and turned away from the windows. Small wonder that I had not awakened earlier. The grey world outside, with the burnt-red roofs climbing the hill, suggested it was not yet morning, but I could see that it was well past dawn. I hurriedly washed in the cold water and dressed in Sister Magdalen's robes, after hesitating a minute or two over the decision. But I reasoned that the innkeeper and his wife had seen me enter as a nun and there would be far too much gossip if I left the inn in a silk gown.

Although I was undoubtedly delaying the three in the next room, I stopped long enough to study my reflection in the window, since there was no mirror or looking glass in the room. I had done the best I could with the materials at hand. I scrubbed my cheeks and my lips to give them colour, but with my hair concealed behind the coif and whatever advantages of figure I might have sufficiently covered by my robes, I presented little temptation to either man.

I opened the door and was slightly shaken to find the voices ceased abruptly and everyone's gaze was fixed on me. I found it hard to guess with what approval or disapproval I was regarded.

I said, 'Good morning, Linette. Paul . . . Captain. I trust you are feeling more the thing this morning, Captain.'

Marius produced a faint voice that announced he was tolerably well, but I could not mistake the mischief in his eyes.

Paul scarcely managed to greet me. He was staring open-mouthed at Sister Magdalen's habit. 'Good God, Clare! This is blasphemous. What are you about?'

'It seemed more correct to travel in this manner, since I am travelling with a gentleman to whom I am not married.'

Surely this should remind him that any earnest fiancé would reveal jealousy, but for Paul the chief difficulty was quite different. 'I suppose it is your affair, but I think it most improper, Clare! I have never approved these Jacobin ideas about religion.'

So it was religion and not jealousy that troubled him. And there, observing it all, were Marius and

Linette. This, I think, was the most maddening factor of all.

A tray had been set upon the table and Paul and Linette both rushed to offer me a mug of something I expected to be chocolate. It was no longer boiling hot, for which I was grateful, but the taste was vile.

'Coffee,' Linette announced proudly. 'Father says it is better for you if you want to start a journey full of fire and spirit. And that it clears the head after a night of – of what, Father?'

'A night of carousing.'

I could well imagine that Marius needed some such remedy after the amount of wine he had consumed the previous night, but he was looking much healthier than he had last night at dinner.

I said, 'Kindly inform your father that I seldom carouse, and I never drink coffee until late afternoon.' It had been all I could do to choke down the first bitter mouthful, and I set the mug back.

Paul apologised for my bad manners to Captain Redon, which I found violently annoying, but Linette ignored him and started to repeat to Marius the entire contents of my little speech. There was newly baked bread on the tray, so I broke off a piece and chewed it, highly conscious of Linette's father watching me as he got into his greatcoat across the room. He laughed at Linette's careful words and answered in the same vein, 'Kindly inform Sister Clare that this is a fast day for one who has taken the veil. She is very fortunate to be offered coffee.'

I joined in his laughter, much to Paul's surprise. I tried to take my defeat in good order, pouring more coffee and drinking it with the bread. I ate hastily, aware that everyone else was dressed for travel, and asked Linette if she would fetch my cloak and my small valise. Paul reached for the cloak but Linette had stepped between us and it was Marius who wrapped the cloak around me. We were very close for a second or two when neither of us moved, but slow as Paul might be, he was not blind.

'Clare, I must speak to you alone. We have matters to discuss.'

Marius apologetically interfered with his plan. 'I very much fear we will have to postpone your little talk, Citizen. You see, we've only a few minutes before the local diligence from Joigny to Lyon makes up its waybill. If we do not book our places, we will have to rent another gig and another horse. And they are not that plentiful.'

'The one we arrived in is already on its way back to that village,' Linette put in. 'So we have to go now.'

Paul was magnanimous. He strode to the door. 'I'll run down and book our places.'

'No!' I cried, then glanced at Marius and bit my lip.

I think he understood the necessity of keeping Paul with us, for he said quickly, 'We may as well leave together. Come, Linette. By the way, Vallier, I assume you intend to accompany us over the French Alps into Italy.'

'I was asked by my patroness to persuade Clare to accompany your daughter. We hardly expected to see you on the journey. Not but what your friends must rejoice in your – er – partial recovery.'

'You are too kind.'

It was I who asked, 'How could you cross the border into France from the Swiss cantons when you are wanted for desertion?'

Paul was offended that no one had told me. 'I am a Swiss citizen now. I should have thought Sylvie would tell you this. Geneva regards me as one of her own. And that will be our future home.

167

I have prospered in my banking connections, thanks to the principessa. Come, we are on our way.'

He may have been prudent in deserting when our fortunes were at a low ebb, and in surrendering the country of his birth for an obviously prospering business in Geneva, but when I compared him with Marius I was deeply ashamed that I had ever had an affection for him.

Paul insisted on taking my arm to escort me down to the coach. It was a little difficult, I had so many robes on. And too, I was perfectly aware that Marius observed every gesture between Paul and me. Was he jealous? I devoutly hoped so.

Nor was I averse to Paul's company for the moment. He seemed immense striding along beside me, a man of power and superb health. He demonstrated this health when we stepped out to the cobbled innyard, inhaling deeply of the cold air, despite the sleet, and announced, 'I am very much in favour of fresh air. I do not feel it detrimental, as so many do. Living in the cantons as I have, I find the pure air efficacious in every way. You should seek more of it, Captain, instead of lying about drinking the wine of the neighbourhood.'

Touché, Captain Redon, I thought with a smile, but of course, Paul rambled on, making things worse. He lowered his bell-like tones slightly. 'Poor devil! I am inclined to offer to escort the child to her Italian estates myself, while this fellow remains here to—'

'Die?' I asked.

'I would not use the word, but anyone may see how ill he is.'

'On the contrary, he looks healthier now than he did the night I first saw him in the Hôtel Dieu in Paris.'

'Well, well, let us hope so. Looks as though he might have an eye for the females. If he offers you

168

any familiarity, you must tell me at once.'

Very carefully, I ventured a side-glance and caught Marius Redon's expression. He had heard every word, I am sure, and looked highly amused. 'Yes, Paul,' I said dutifully. 'I shall tell you at once when the Captain commits some act which I do not invite.'

Linette brought us back to the business at hand by reminding us that the coachman and the other passengers were all gathering around the big, clumsy diligence which seated more than a score of passengers.

It looked to me as though half of Joigny was bound for Lyon on this day. Unfortunately, so was half the livestock of Joigny. Chickens, ducks, geese and one protesting kid were loaded onto the big wagon, to be sold for Christmas feasts in Lyon or nearby towns. It was not long since the excesses of the Terror in Lyon when thousands died under the Law of Suspects, but the human spirit had risen above these horrors and one would never guess, to see these well-fed, quarrelsome, laughing citizens, that they had not always known such optimism.

Only three seats could be booked for us, and those not together. All seats in the big, rocking carriage faced forward, which should help Linette with her motion sickness. Since she had been issued no seat, she claimed as she sat in a gingerly way on Marius' lap that she would cause no more trouble than the loudly bleating kid whose owner sat immediately in front of them. This was not a lucky comparison, as the goat complained all the way to the post stop where we all ate our late supper before the first of two long and painful nights aboard the swaying vehicle.

Paul obligingly let me sleep against his shoulder and I was delighted to see that this arrangement brought a scowl to Marius Redon's face and made Linette confide to me the following morning that her father felt Citizen Vallier was too familiar with me.

'Because of the appearance it makes with my habit and my coif?' I asked innocently.

'It must be that,' she admitted. 'I wonder if Father quite trusts Citizen Vallier.'

I was combing her hair in the Ladies' Retiring Room and the men had already strolled out into the innyard of this ancient town with its medieval round towers and narrow, tortuous streets.

I said, 'We must never let him out of our sight. I hope your father knows that. We have one more long drive and then Lyon. Once we transfer to the Alpine Coach it will surely be too late for him to send messages to the princess.'

'Unless,' Linette said wisely, 'one of the princess' people is in Lyon, waiting to take the coach with us.'

But I couldn't believe it of Paul. He was too ingenuous. He looked back at the inn now, flashing his wide-mouthed grin, and he made some motion which caused Linette to murmur, 'Heavens! He is blowing you a kiss. I thought he was stroking that funny moustache. Are you actually going to marry him?'

'He is quite sure of it,' I said.

So absolutely certain of everything was my betrothed that he had not once on the trip asked me what my own feelings were. He had talked only of the future, after I had earned two hundred English pounds for delivering Linette to her family, and he and I would then return to the Swiss cantons where he had certain business connections, among them the influence of the principessa's friends in Geneva. 'Once this girl is delivered to her family,' he assured me confidently, 'she will very soon grow to love her great-grandmother and the rest of them. Sylvie tells me that the princess is of the very ancient nobility.'

I said to Linette now, 'I haven't the least notion what your father intends to do with you in Italy. Restore you to your estates, of course, but how he thinks to keep the princess' hands off, I have no notion.'

She shrugged. 'He says there are good Viscontis. They aren't all villians and abductors.' But she seemed curiously indifferent about the whole thing.

And so, at mid-Christmas Day, we arrived in the great east-central city of Lyon, once the head-quarters of the French silk industry which had been denounced as anti-revolutionary and was only now coming back to life. General Bonaparte was urging the ladies of good families to return to Lyon silk but rumour had it that his wife and spoiled beauties like Thérèse Tallien persisted in wearing their English muslins. As a merchant in the diligence remarked upon entering Lyon, 'The General may give us a sound government, but he can't give his wife sound principles.'

I found my fellow passengers' criticisms of the city's roads, shops and inns exaggerated. To me, the joining of the two rivers, the Rhone and the Saône, had formed a city of a mysterious and reserved charm. It was not a city for gaiety, but it was sombrely elegant, its narrow streets lined by fine, old, secretive-looking houses, and it was no dirtier than Paris. The banks of the Rhone provided openness and the river gave light and sparkle to the sober city.

I did think, however, that it was a perfect city for conspiracies and for danger. Were the princi-pessa's agents waiting for us somewhere on these secretive streets? I had still learned nothing suspicious from Paul and was coming to the conclusion that he had been honest in his ignorance of the old woman's plans. Certainly he mentioned her every hour or so, praising her wisdom and emphasising that she could help him and 'his betrothed' when we married and went to live in Geneva.

When we descended from the diligence and our fellow passengers scattered with their livestock, I informed my comrades that I did not intend to carry on the irreverent masquerade as Sister Clare. I was promptly reminded by Linette that my passport papers were made out in the name of Sister Magdalen Marie. I laughed at the absurdity of our little group. 'And very shortly, Paul, your papers will be examined, too. You cannot possibly have entered France under your own name. What is your masquerade?'

He said stiffly, 'I do not regard myself as a traitor. I was – I am an émigré. I entered France to assist you, because Sylvie felt that my presence would make your duty easier for you. And too, she feared that our long separation might have made you doubt my devotion. But she did not in the least know you, my dear. That was absurd, of course.'

'Of course,' I agreed. Marius looked at me, but I stared innocently at the threatening sky and suggested that we get inside at once before we drowned in the coming cloudburst. Marius drew up the collar of his greatcoat, pulled down the brim of his beaver hat, and took my arm before Paul could do so.

'And none too soon,' Marius said, beckoning Linette to his other side.

Paul was beside us in two strides. 'Now, see here! I think we had best . . .'

'Where are we to stay until the Mont Cenis Coach departs?' I cut in, hoping to soothe Paul. I certainly wanted no quarrelling between the men. It would take little more to bring about our betrayal, if Paul felt himself slighted in some way.

Paul accepted this question as addressed to him

and was describing an inn called, he thought, The Loyal Lyonnaise, when Marius agreed with such enthusiasm that I was at once suspicious, although I said nothing.

'I know the place. The very place. We leave the quai and the river here and turn up that byway there.'

'Really.' Paul surveyed the streets, almost concealed by the misty rain. 'I should have thought it was much nearer the innyard where they make up the coach.'

I said to Paul suddenly, 'Where did you stay when you came through here a few days ago?'

'But that very inn, The Loyal Lyonnaise.'

Marius nudged me. I said nothing, but I was quite certain Marius had no intention of leading us to Paul's inn. If Paul should prove to be betraying us, what could be easier than that he should lead us directly into a trap arranged several days ago and awaiting our arrival? But how could he know we would be arriving together, or that he would meet us as he had? That meeting was purely fortuitous, an accident, I would swear to that!

Twice I looked back. Both times I saw indistinct figures walking in our direction but in both cases they turned off, leaving us alone again.

The rain was coming down in great sheets by the time we reached an inn within sight of the Alpine Coach's current point of departure somewhat east of the Place Bellecour, the central square.

'This is not the place,' Paul complained. 'It was closer to the innyard where we are to take the coach.' But both Linette and I were soaked through and we shared an unspoken anxiety about Marius who was a trifle grim and had that white look around his mouth again.

'Let us go in here,' I said after a signal from Marius, 'or we will drown in the streets.'

173

'Yes. Do! I insist!' Paul surprised me by agreeing. 'These ladies are wet through.'

Marius apologised for having led us astray but agreed that Paul was entirely in the right. We should accept this inn and forget the vain search for The Loyal Lyonnaise.

What a wily rogue Marius is, I thought. He had manoeuvred us away from Paul's choice and made Paul himself insist on it. But I was greatly thankful for that quality in Marius. We all hurried inside and then, as I felt the ugly slap-slap of soggy skirts against my petticoats, I remembered my position and slowed to a stately walk, more suitable to Sister Magdalen Marie. The public room was at the end of the dark little entrance foyer, with the taprail closer to the entry, while the fireplace was so crowded with midday Christmas celebrants, there was clearly no room for newcomers.

Paul announced generously that he would handle the matter of quarters in which we might change and dry out our saturated clothing, while awaiting the late afternoon departure of the Alpine Coach for the dreaded Mont Cenis Pass. Marius had already removed Linette's greatcoat, and I was shaking it when Paul came back with the landlord. Paul explained, a trifle out of sorts, as he saw Marius removing my own cape, 'The good man declares there is no room here, except to officers and men of the Army.'

'The Patriot Army,' the landlord corrected him sharply. 'I can always find space for members of our glorious army. You – Citizen – ' He addressed Marius but seemed to find it hard to believe him. 'The citizen says you are of the army?'

'Captain Redon, currently on the service of the First Consul, General Bonaparte. At your service, Patriot.'

This changed the complexion of the affair. I

worried briefly because Marius had given his true name, but by this time if anyone were inquiring for our group, our identity would be pretty obvious anyway. And there was always my honest betrothed, Paul Vallier. He was sure to tell anyone and everyone who asked.

'I can give you my back parlour for the afternoon,' the patriotic innkeeper agreed. 'It is my daughter's parlour, but she is away with her husband's family in Arney le Duc.' He added with pride, 'Her husband is with the Grenadier Guard.'

Paul raised his chin and started to utter those words 'my own outfit' which make common denominators for so many, but he recalled in time that he had deserted when the army was raw, inexperienced, and barefoot. It must be painful to witness pride in a group of men he had despised. But he was a Geneva businessman now. Perhaps he really didn't care any more.

We dripped the entire length of the passage to the back parlour, a cosy little room with a roaring fire, almost too hot with its red portières, red chair coverings and a scarlet carpet. It was decided that Linette and I should change while the men dried off as best they could among the Christmas celebrants in the public room. Because of our concern for Marius, Linette and I accomplished our change within minutes, but fortunately, Paul and Marius made their own changes within the taproom, and doubtless with the help of the two tapster's girls. Marius had exhausted his supply of shirts, but managed to purchase two slightly too frilly ones, from a drunken dandy. Paul, ever prepared for what was correct, had no problem.

Shortly after noon we ordered dinner, seeing that Marius looked haggard and was not adding much to the chatter of Linette and Paul. These two had found a subject in common. Both liked mountain climbing.

'Not that I ever climbed anything higher than Mt Ste Geneviève in the Latin Quarter,' Linette said. 'But I know I would love walking. I like to travel. I haven't been sick since the first night on the coach.'

Paul talked of the mountains in the cantons, and then of his great success in Geneva, something about money exchanges made with the aid of the Milanese principessa. I glanced over at Marius. He had closed his eyes, and with his legs stretched straight out before him, he appeared to be asleep, but he winced and his mouth twisted a little. His wound must have been troubling him. I wondered what we could do to help him.

Then the dinner arrived. Marius waved away any food but drank a glass of wine. The preparation of the local river fish was delicious, tender and moist, in a lightly flavoured sauce. The Christmas goose was a trifle fat, but one could not expect miracles, and the brandied cake made Linette so happy she fell asleep almost as soon as the tray had been cleared away. Even Paul remarked sleepily, 'The Alpine Coach leaves in mid-afternoon. Let us not forget. However . . .' He yawned and massaged his moustache sleepily.

I also was tired, but I knew we must be ready for the Coach within two hours at the most. Nonetheless, it was excessively comfortable here . . .

With an enormous effort I moved my head, first astonished, then terrified at my weakness. I tried to call out, but I lacked the strength. My eyes appeared to close of their own volition. The warm darkness invited me.

CHAPTER TWELVE

I CAME to consciousness to find myself being shaken until my teeth chattered. I opened my eyes painfully. My limbs nearly collapsed under me, for I seemed to be walking up and down across the scarlet carpet. Someone was groaning. That was Linette, rubbing her head and complaining that she was thirsty. The innkeeper and half the patrons were crowded around the girl, shocked, and offering her help that she did not seem to want or require. As for me, Marius had his arm around me, one hand on each of my shoulders. I turned my head. My lips touched his bare throat. His clothes looked disordered, as though he had been wrestling with me. Perhaps he had! I mumbled an apology, finding it hard to speak.

His tired, tense expression softened. 'Good! You sound more yourself now.'

'You shook me!'

This time he laughed. 'But my darling girl, you were poisoned. All of you. It is fortunate I had no appetite. Now, if you are feeling better, we will work upon your beloved.'

'My beloved?'

'Citizen Vallier.'

'Oh,' I said. Embarrassingly enough, I had forgotten all about him. Poor man. His friends poisoned him with as little compunction as they showed in trying to poison Marius, Linette, and me.

177

'Was it deliberate?' I whispered. Marius nodded, adding, 'It is common knowledge by this time. I was desperate for help. I had to tell them I suspected laudanum.'

'From whom?'

'Unknown agents of the Royalists, of course.'

'Dastardly villains!' the innkeeper cried, hearing our conversation. 'Royalists! Émigrés, all of them. How is the poor gentleman? Ah! Coming around, I see. Well, Citizen,' he said to the dazed Paul, 'this is what comes of your having too large an appetite. You eat royalist poisons, as well!'

To Marius I murmured with indignation, 'Are we to let this poisoner escape as the principessa's little man escaped punishment in Paris?'

'Come.' His order made me recall suddenly that he was used to issuing orders. With an arm around my waist he took me over to the window and drew the portière aside. The oiled paper window had long ago been destroyed by weathering but the shutter was warped so badly I could witness a ghastly scene out in the narrow alley that wound its way up an incline behind the inn. The alley was running with rainwater, and the rain itself beat down upon the body of a young woman. Several townsmen gathered to watch two uniformed National Guardsmen lift the girl.

I gasped. 'What has happened to her? Is she dead?'

'The cook, the innkeeper and the tapsters all swear she was talking with a little man. A lean dark little man.'

'Ridetti?'

'He was hanging about when our tray was made up. A bribe, perhaps. Afterward, she was found out there. She seems to have been struck a killing blow across the nape of the neck. It may be that she was struck by a cart or a tumbrel. But – '

'But probably by Ridetti – or whoever it was – afterward.'

'Just so.'

'What are we to do?'

He drew me further into the dusty portières so that there was no possibility of our being heard. 'I have an idea. Would you consider leaving your friend – that is to say, your betrothed – here to recover while we rattle off to Mont Cenis, but not in the Alpine Coach?'

'What! You *are* Machiavellian. Are we making hire of a private coach? That would be prohibitive.'

'No. But we are to take the evening coach crossing the French Alps, meeting the Mont Cenis Coach at the inn, if there are no storms.'

It was a large 'if' but I had gambled this far and, in any case, I knew I would go with them.

'What must we do?'

'You are sicker than you appear. We decide we cannot leave today. Then, at the last minute, we arrive at the innyard where the Landsel Coach makes up. There will be only four other passengers if the Coach is fully booked. It leaves three hours after the regular Alpine Coach. And in any case, we do the unexpected.'

'But who will book our passage?'

He smiled. 'The tapster. I was talking with him earlier, told him I was in love with you. He understood perfectly. He is not a man of religion and the fact that you are a nun did not trouble him in the slightest. He said I was a true revolutionary.'

'Heavens!'

'Not precisely. At all events, I told him that Vallier was a Swiss banker, removing his child from contact with Jacobin France. The tapster is already on our side.'

I rolled my eyes but I was amused even through

179

the weakness and the headache I felt from the drugged food.

'Why did they drug us? None of us died.'

He glanced at the excitement around Paul Vallier, who was coming to himself. Linette sat apart from the others, closer to us. Marius had evidently warned her. She appeared to be sleepy, only half-aware of what went on. As Marius talked to me, he continued to watch her to be certain she was safe.

'I imagine it was intended that when we were unconscious, Linette and I, at least, would be killed.'

He told me again, carefully, of his plans, but I was still confused, my head ached like the great clangours of Notre Dame, and I merely agreed to do whatever I was told. Then I went over and did what I could to soothe Paul. I suggested we pay for a bed to be brought into this parlour where he could recuperate. He had eaten so much more of the brandied cake than Linette and I that he was in very poor condition to travel anywhere, for according to the innkeeper, the cake was the culprit in our poisoning.

I reassured Paul that we would not be leaving until he and Linette recovered, feeling guilty as I lied to him, but his persistence in believing everything Sylvie and the princess told him had awakened me to the fact that he was a stupid man. I pitied him for his innocence and worse, his ignorance. I wondered if I would have lost all feeling for him except pity, if he had married me long ago, or if I had never met Marius Redon.

Since the girl who put the laudanum drops in the cake had been killed, probably by Ridetti, we would still be watched. Someone among the crowd who had seen us was certain to relay the news that the attempt had failed; so with the aid of Linette, who was clearly born to be an actress, we exaggerated the plight of a sick man, a sick child, myself with a raging headache, and Marius trying in vain to help us all recover. For the further benefit of the audience, Marius haggled with the innkeeper to let us all remain here overnight and possibly longer, until the next Alpine Coach set out.

When we were alone, with Paul well wrapped and shivering by the fire, Linette made a great deal of noise, talking, groaning, complaining, to drown out the low-voiced plans made by Marius and me as we stood at the old scarlet portières, pretending to look out at the lowering weather.

'Do not change back to the nun's habit,' he instructed me, 'until we are approaching the last post before the border. We must leave by a cart provided by the tapster.'

'Can we trust him?'

'I believe so. His patriotism seems genuine, and he is particularly anxious to outwit Vallier. He once worked for a Swiss at Berne and it seems the fellow was close-fisted.'

'It takes a rogue to know a rogue,' I said, and Marius did not disagree. Then he glanced at Linette and back to me. The amusement was gone.

'You have risked much for Linette and me, much more than I ever dreamed when I supposed I was dying. I can never repay you.'

I said casually, 'We will think of some payment, I daresay.'

'I daresay.' He surprised me by kissing me suddenly, this time on the lips. I was so surprised that I did not have time to enjoy the kiss while it lasted, but as soon as I recovered, I said, 'I see you intend to play your game of hearts with me.'

'I couldn't resist,' he explained in his teasing way. 'You looked so kissable.'

'I must husband my money if I am always to be paid in such coin.'

But unlike Paul who had never known, Marius

understood when I was joking and when I was not. His arm tightened about my waist, but neither of us said anything more for the moment. I knew that he and I had more urgent concerns.

I said, 'They will be expecting a nun in a habit and coif. Those people out there celebrating – good Lord! It is Christmas!'

'They won't see us, darling. We will be leaving by the tapster's cart. I sincerely hope.' There was a little break in his voice, then he said quietly, 'A Merry Christmas, Clare Dubeque. It will never be Clare Vallier, will it?'

'Probably not.'

'Good. Clare Vallier. There is no ring to it. It doesn't suit you at all.'

'How good of you to say so! I will keep your opinion in mind, Captain.'

It was not difficult for Linette to pretend, for the benefit of the patrons at the inn, that she was still quite ill. Her stomach troubled her, and she suffered from a headache. We both sat near Paul on his couch at the fire, speaking of the night and the following day, as though we would spend this time in Lyon. Marius obliged Paul by inquiring if he knew how often the Alpine Coach made its way from Lyon over the Alps to Milano. We believed we had convinced Paul that we would not be leaving the city until the next coach.

Unexpectedly, Paul betrayed the fact that he had been paid to make the trip into France with his new Swiss papers. 'But only to assist you, Clare, you understand that. The Viscontis have money invested in Geneva. One of the principessa's grand-children gave me my instructions. I was to persuade you to make this trip. Captain, would you throw that log onto the grate? Sorry, I know you are not in the best of health, but you will appreciate my own difficulties.'

While Marius was obliging him, Paul shivered in his blanket and I tucked him in more carefully while Linette took a bowl of broth from the innkeeper, then set it back on the tray.

'You taste it, Citizen.'

'You permit.' The innkeeper obligingly took a spoon to at least a quarter of the bowl and then gave the remainder to Linette, who offered it to me with a feeble groan, 'You feed it to him. I'm terribly sick.'

I was worried until I saw her little wink. Satisfied that between them, Linette and Marius would see us through, I fed Paul the broth. His teeth chattered against the spoon, but presently he finished the bowl, and prompted by my questions, explained why he had been paid by the principessa's agents.

'To see to the safety of yourself and the child, of course. At least, that was my understanding. But it seemed that there was some question of whether you would actually set out or not, and I was to persuade you. Not that I need have done so. I know you well enough, Clare, to believe that had I explained the importance of your taking the child across the Alps, you would have done as I asked.'

How innocent men are, I thought, and had the satisfaction of seeing him sleep presently, quite content with the world.

By this time Linette came back to tap my shoulder. 'It is done,' she whispered. 'And we've a splendid basket of food. Father paid the tapster, and his wife made it. No one else knows. It's in the cart. Are you ready? I met his wife. She cried over me. She said she had a child who would have been my age, but he died at birth. Isn't it odd to cry after so long? Well, are you ready?'

I looked back at Paul, suddenly feeling my guilt at deserting the sick man. But I thought of the

183

efforts to kill Linette and Marius, and the fact that Paul was deeply involved with the Viscontis.

'One moment. I want to be certain he has plenty of money with him. He must have enough to pay his reckoning and to take him wherever he chooses to go.'

I needn't have troubled. Paul had enough silver, and some gold pieces, to get him to Paris, or to Geneva. I replaced them in the pockets of his waistcoat beneath his outer coat.

Marius put Sister Magdalen's short cloak around my shoulders, over my silk gown. I had not pelisse or coat of my own. No one was in the back of the passage when we hurried out through the rear door. A cart loaded with logs and an assortment of stones stood close by the door. Our friend, the tapster, was on the box. He was a dim, indistinct figure through the rainy dusk, but the dimness would help to conceal us. Marius lifted Linette into the back of the cart, then, as she scrambled to lie flat among the stones, he lifted me up beside her. When he swung in after us, and pulled a heavy sailcloth over us, we laughed silently at each other as we flattened out among the tapster's choice objects of concealment.

It seemed no time before the cart had rattled around the narrow alley onto an unpaved street, and suddenly the ancient nag came to a halt before an innyard so ill-lighted we could scarcely see each other as we dropped off the end of the cart. The tapster – bless him – came around to the three of us with the huge basket and our valises.

'I could not book the four forward seats, but those opposite are yours. There are only four other passengers.'

'How can we thank you?' I asked with all my heart.

'It was nothing, Citizeness. The Captain paid for your food, and there is nothing I enjoy more than to aid a good brace of patriots. Especially against a Swiss banker.'

Marius thanked him again, Linette kissed him on the cheek, and I said to him at the last second, 'Please be kind to the gentleman at the inn. Let him go his way when he is well. But do not, for the love of God, tell him where we have gone.'

'I will ignore him. It is best. Here is your coach, exactly on the hour of darkness as promised.'

He was correct. He had barely got his cart and horse out of the way when the Landsel Coach and team roared out of the cobbled yard on its Christmas night journey. The other passengers were already seated as we took our places. First impressions on such occasions are invariably grim, especially in the flicker of light from the carriage lamps. We were therefore relieved when the four persons staring at us were introduced to us by the coachman, who smelled strongly of spirits, as a young bride and groom, a widow carrying her late husband to burial in his native Torino, and a handsome blond boy a little older than Linette who caught her interest immediately.

Our unspoken question was answered by the blond boy who said in a perfectly audible whisper, 'The coffin is on the roof. It has been booked at the price of a regular passenger.'

While everyone else seemed interested in Linette's conversation with the talkative blond boy who sat opposite her beside the door, Marius murmured to me, 'We are this far, in any case.' He had my hand in his, and it was a moment of pleasure and content-ment. I nodded.

'Halfway there, don't you think?'

He did not disagree, but of course, we both knew the most dangerous sector of the journey would be over the great passes of the Alps. As to the other danger, that from the principessa, we could only hope for the best. I looked across the coach toward the window. Because of the fantastic view of the Alps which even I, who did not usually travel, had heard about, the curtains to the windows could be pulled back and fastened during the daylight hours. In the early evening dark, I could see only distant flickers of light between the curtains which had not been entirely closed.

'In other circumstances, I might have liked Lyon,' I said.

Marius smiled. 'As for me, I can never entirely dislike any of this trip.' He closed his eyes. I was quiet then. He must have been under great strain, with all the physical exertions of the day, his attempts to rouse Linette and me from the drug, and later, transporting us from the inn to the coach. I suppose I was used to seeing that look about his eyes from the pain his injury gave him from time to time, so when the yellow-haired little bride leaned forward and touched my knee, I was surprised at first by what she was saying.

She whispered in a shy, breathy voice, 'Your husband is not well? Perhaps the sway of the coach troubles him. I know how that is. I am often affected exactly so. But my dear Albert is such a comfort.' She hugged her bridegroom who looked suitably puffed with pride and a smug sense of his importance on this occasion.

It was almost on my tongue to say quickly that it was a war injury which troubled Marius, but fortunately, his clasp tightened on my fingers and I caught myself in time. The less they knew about us, the better. I agreed with the bride. 'My poor husband is never a good traveller, I fear. Our son is much the best traveller of the family.'

Although Marius' eyes remained closed, a flicker at the corner of his lips told me that he heard and was amused.

With the coach on its way and all three of us safe for the moment, I could sit back and be grateful that we had not taken the regular Alpine Coach. These passengers seemed reasonably pleasant, not at all the sort we had found in the employ of the princess.

After our first night on the Landsel-Mont Cenis Coach we were sure that this trip would be more comfortable than those nights in the crowded diligence from Joigny to Lyon. For one thing, the two young people, although restless and constantly on the move, still occupied very little room as we all tried to sleep. The widow took out her frilled black nightcap, set it jauntily over her greying curls, and after dabbing at her eyes with her lace-bordered black handkerchief, she snored off to sleep.

The bride and groom were presented with greater problems but seemed able to surmount them with aplomb. They both produced sleeping robes, his of figured satin, hers of unpatriotic muslin trimmed in fur, an absurd combination of which she was extremely proud. Marius and I were requested to keep our eyes closed as the newlyweds removed their heavy outer garments and replaced them with these festive robes. Afterward, they curled up in one corner of the coach, and somewhat to my surprise, at once went off to sleep.

Marius and I exchanged a few cynically amused comments on 'post-revolutionary' love, but eventually, we also slept.

It was my turn to be embarrassed in the dark, rainy morning. Though Linette had curled up rigidly in her corner and was dreaming a very pleasant dream, with her greatcoat over her and a smile on her mobile face, I found myself sharing Marius' travel cloak, with my head cushioned against his shoulder and his arm around me. We awoke at the same time and before I could move, he was smoothing the tousled hair out of my eyes with his thumb and forefinger. I felt for the first time in six years what it was to know a gesture of such tenderness, and I was tongue-tied.

Then I remembered that this position could not be very pleasant for a man who, until recently, had been expected to die in the Hôtel Dieu. I wanted to ask him how he could endure so much. I knew he suffered considerable pain and discomfort; that was no pretence. But was this a man who had been dying only a week ago? Yet how could I ask him such a question? He was a very mysterious man.

Linette's boyish friend awoke a few minutes later, and kicked at Linette's boot soles to arouse her as well. Marius and I were interested in his efforts, wondering if he had suspected Linette was a girl. The fact that he kicked her boots did not seem to me very romantic, and I was of the opinion that he did not yet know her sex. Linette awoke, stretched, grinned at the boy and announced, 'I'm hungry.'

Marius, the boy and I all laughed, unintentionally awakening the bride and groom and finally the widow.

Any sensuous ideas that either the bride and groom or Marius and I might have had were effectively scotched by the widow's thoughtful remark, as she removed her nightcap. 'I do hope Gaston was not disturbed by this dreadful downpour.'

'Gaston?' asked the bride confusedly. She had only just come out of her Albert's arms. I understood very well her confusion.

The widow explained with a hint of surprise, 'But my husband, of course. Gaston. He is on the roof and I trust the coffin will not warp with all this rain.'

The weather did not improve during the day, and according to the posts where we frequently stopped for the teams to be changed or for the coachman to take a 'drop of spirits,' there was not much prospect of anything better once we reached the Italian border. We were told a heavy snowfall was expected. The Alpine passes were blocked in the east, but as yet, the high, narrow passages in the western Alps were not impassable.

What would happen if we were delayed in getting Linette to her mysterious family in Milano? That family to which Marius was entrusting his daughter. Were they not connected most intimately with the principessa? I still did not know why Marius would trust one branch of the family when he suspected its ancient head of being a potential murderess.

No difficulties presented themselves as our coach climbed ever higher into the mountains, and we three became lighthearted, almost forgetting our fears, and the physical barriers awaiting us over the border. By the time we were approaching the famed Mont Cenis Pass, we were even joking among ourselves about the coffin on the roof of the coach. On the day we reached the last post on the French side of the border, the snow was piled so high on both sides of the road that we could scarcely see the little mountainside inn, though the weather was momentarily sunny.

We took my valise in with us. By the looking glass in the chamber used by the old innkeeper's wife, I intended to change to the coif and habit of Sister Magdalen. It would shock our fellow travellers, but not quite as much as my appearance without it, when my passport papers proclaimed me Sister Magdalen Marie.

I opened the valise, tossed aside the extra petticoat and shift, the extra changes for Linette, and found nothing. I turned it upside down on the heavy alcove bed and scrambled through the contents. Had I forgotten to pack the clothing myself? But I recalled every move, the way I had smoothed and folded the newly dried and ironed garments and put them into the bottom of the valise, then folded and placed Linette's extra clothing on top. That valise had gone directly to the Landsel Coach.

But which of those passengers, or the coachman or the postilion who had acted as coachman during the latter's rest periods, had taken Sister Magdalen's clothing? I hadn't noticed either the coachman or the postilion, except that they were not averse to strong spirits.

I knew why the garments had been taken. It was an attempt to cause me trouble in crossing the border. But it was sinister too. It told me that the principessa's long tentacles had reached out to coil around us again. We had not lost her at all.

CHAPTER THIRTEEN

I WENT out to the public room, but the air outside was so cold that I found almost everyone, including the widow, Linette, and her young friend, Raoul, at the taprail. I didn't like to disturb Marius. He had slouched into a chair in the corner with his head back, and a mug of something amber-coloured – hot brandy perhaps – in his hand. The mug was tilted between his fingers. A few drops had spilled out.

Linette and the boy were playing some kind of game. They had been given mugs of heated liquor and it was clear that the boy had drunk far too much, or too rapidly. He was using great, sweeping gestures punctuated by obnoxious boasts. Quite unlike the gentlemanly appearance he had presented in the coach.

I questioned Linette quietly about her own drink, but I was relieved to find that hers was chiefly hot water. Linette confided, 'Father mixed the drink for me.'

'Is he feeling ill?' I asked. If he were to relapse into the weakened state in which I had first met him, there was little we could do. There was surely no surgeon, nor even any other habitation, within more than a day's ride. Undoubtedly this sudden rise in altitude, along with the bitter cold, had reacted upon him.

Linette's friend Raoul interrupted us flippantly, 'Léon, do you know, you aren't the least like your mother. The Citizeness is a beauty. And I see now her eyes are gold . . . no, gold and brown. Your father too has brown eyes. But your eyes are blue.'

The youth was very close to Linette. I felt that he knew she was a girl in spite of that lean, boyish look of hers. And I began to wonder if he had some sinister reason for keeping silent about his knowledge. I turned away from him and from the taprail, gesturing for Linette to follow me.

As we moved, Raoul swung around, grinning. 'The Citizeness needn't run away, merely because a gentleman took a fancy to her eyes. I mean her no harm. I'll do her a deal of good.'

Linette whispered anxiously. 'He really does mean you no harm . . . Mother. He is only teasing.'

'His teasing is too adult for his years. I think he must be unused to spirits.'

I had moved away from the chattering group at the taprail to avoid the boy's insolent eyes and to speak in private to Linette, but unhappily, this placed us nearer Marius and must have called the boy's attention to him. Raoul reached for my arm, caught at my sleeve and tore it slightly.

'Here, now, Cit—Citizeness, you'll get no help from that one you're yoked to. He's dead to this world. But me – I'm not so young as I may look.' He took a step, and as Linette started to protest, he seized my wrist in a surprisingly strong grip. 'Try me, beauti—beautiful Citizeness . . . ' I winced, snatched my hand away as he took another step and tried to seize me in his arms. A second later he stumbled over Marius' suddenly outstretched boot, fell and sprawled flat upon the floor. So Marius had been aware of everything that went on!

Linette was very much concerned about all of us, but she knelt and tried to help the youth to his feet. He furiously shook her off. Not looking back, he stalked away, brushing himself as he went. Unfortunately, he must have been all too aware of the chuckles from the rest of the group leaning against the taprail.

Marius looked up at me. 'I can't find it in my heart to blame the lad for his good taste. You are beautiful after all.'

Nevertheless, it was the first such attention I'd had in several years. I could not prevent myself from asking him now, 'Does the pain trouble you so very much? Isn't there something I can do?'

He no longer made any effort to hide it. 'You can pray we reach our destination before this carcass quits me. Or you may damn the excellent marksmanship of the Austrian whose rifle did the damage.'

I don't know why the remark passed me by without question. I suppose I was concerned over so many things.

Linette wanted to fuss over him, but I coaxed her away. I got a fresh mug of brandy with a little water. The drink was still steaming. I brought it over to Marius, and he gazed at me briefly as he raised the fresh mug to his lips. I felt in his look that I had been rewarded.

Meanwhile, however, there was the important fact of the missing habit and coif. I couldn't worry Marius with it at the moment, so I called Linette away to the fire at the other end of the public room, and told her what had happened.

'But Clare, you must have forgotten to pack them. Remember? They had to be dried and an iron put to them. Couldn't you have forgotten? We were in such a hurry when we left Lyon.'

'No, I remember quite clearly. Linette, I didn't want to lay this problem upon your shoulders but I don't like to disturb your father.'

'Me, I'm an old campaigner.' Then she muttered, uneasily, 'I wish Father hadn't been forced to trip up Raoul. Now Raoul may be angry, and we will have another enemy.'

I agreed silently, but all the same, I was profoundly grateful for Marius' intervention.

'Which of them is it then?' I asked, partly of Linette, partly of myself. 'The postilion? He has a rogue's face, but that seems a hard judgement. I've never noticed him hanging about the luggage, especially our valises.'

I glanced over at the group across the room. The lanky postilion was eating white cheese and bread between pulls on a straw-covered bottle. Our coachman, a heavy, grizzled fellow, was staring sleepily into his brandy mug, which did not augur well for the next stretch of our journey. He seemed oblivious to the efforts being made by our widow to strike up a conversation with him.

'Have you thought of her?' Linette asked me, following my glance.

'The widow?'

'Watch her when she walks. Very heavy steps. Not gliding, like a woman used to long, full gowns. Not like you, or the bride, for example. What a little silly she is!'

'The widow?' I asked, confused.

'No, no. The bride. Over there drinking out of one cup, and kissing. Wet, noisy kisses . . . Ugh!'

I laughed, but our problem hadn't been solved and I was still greatly troubled, not only about which of those fellow travellers had removed the habit and coif, but what I would do when we reached the border station.

I went back to the now icy room where I had unpacked the valise. I put everything in order, and started out the door, only to find the stout widow in the doorway. Had she been watching me? The precise grey curls peeking out coyly around her bonnet and voluminous black veil seemed to bob up and down, as she asked me in an embarrassed whisper, 'Can you tell me, dear child, where I may find the – er – powdering closet?'

I hadn't heard that expression since hair powdering became a swift route to the guillotine. Trying not to smile, I pointed to the heavy door at the end of the passage. 'There is a water closet in a shed attached to the chalet, just beyond that door. I'm afraid it's very cold out there.'

But I needn't have worried. She invariably wore her black gloves, and everything else about her person was heavily wrapped in funereal black. She was warm enough. Through her veil I could see her eyelids flutter in embarrassment. She walked away, as Linette had said, with larger strides than I might have taken. It was a small matter upon which to build suspicion and I tried to recall what her face looked like on those occasions when her veils were pushed aside, but there had always been the deep shadow of her bonnet. Still . . .

I pretended to be adjusting the clothing in my valise until the door opened, and the widow tracked in snow upon the ancient carpeting. She seemed in excellent spirits, but she was certainly startled when I stepped in her way.

'Well,' I said, 'I seem to have everything in order at last. I must say, I admire your courage in travelling alone so soon after your bereavement, Citizeness.'

'Please – I am old now. That word is harsh upon my poor old ears. I was Madame Lallequin for so very long. Yes, it asks courage to travel alone, but one does what one must. Poor Louis! He never did like cold weather.'

Louis.

He had been Gaston when she was worrying over his warped coffin. An interesting slip. Of course, Linette had slipped in calling me Clare, but then, we were masquerading also. I said with my friendliest, most confidential air, 'You were married long then. How romantic! I do envy you. And you are travelling all the way to Milano?'

But she was on guard and very careful this time. 'To Torino, my dear. My husband's birthplace.'

'Ah yes, of course. Still, it is none so distant in open weather. We shall undoubtedly see you shopping in Milano from time to time. And you must call upon us.'

'No!' she said with unexpected sharpness. 'Not Milano!' She added, 'I thought you were French.'

'I am. But one of my dearest friends lives just outside Milano, the Principessa Visconti. Her château, indeed, her castle, is as well-known as that of the Sforzas.'

The Widow Lallequin was a little flustered. 'Now that you remind me, I do recall . . . a great family during the Middle Ages, I believe. You are to stay there?'

'Is it not generous of her? But yes. She and I became great intimates in Paris and I am in expectation of meeting her almost from moment to moment. At all events, in Milano. So you see, my invitation was not a mere politeness.'

'Ah!' She still seemed confused, as well she might! A footstep behind me from the taproom made her lower her voice, but she was perfectly audible in her excitement. 'Then I understand I am to meet you and the principessa at her château very shortly. It is settled.'

She hurried past me, muttering, 'Pardon, Monsieur.' A few steps beyond, and I turned to follow her. Marius Redon stood there looking at me with a kind of burning in his eyes, the rest of his face too pale to read in this ill-lighted passage. For a moment it seemed perfectly clear to me that he would understand my speaking with the woman, that I had only been sounding her out, and I started to explain. I had got out several words when I realised that the widow had said something to me which destroyed all his confidence in me and turned any affection into something akin to hatred. What had the woman said? Or what had I said that was so disastrous? Something about meeting at the principessa's château. But he must know it was only playacting.

I said quickly, 'Someone has stolen my habit and coif. I was spying, trying to discover if the widow was the principessa's agent. I believe she is. You did understand what I was doing, didn't you?'

'I understood perfectly. You were a charming spy,' he agreed, but the iciness was not far to seek behind the compliment. 'And now, I imagine we have an explanation of why your betrothed happened upon us by purest chance in Joigny. I wondered about that. I was blind enough to believe it actually was chance. But, of course, he *boasted* of his patroness, the Princess Visconti. You were a trifle more shy of such boasting.'

The coachman's voice bellowed through the little inn, 'Landsel Coach! Taking up all passengers. Citizens! Landsel Coach departs at once!'

'But my habit! My coif! They've been stolen!' I cried, abandoning my defence in this more immediate concern.

'I don't in the least doubt you will find a way to fool the guards. You have a masterly talent for deception.'

I was hurt and shocked, but I was angry too. He had no faith in me. Worst of all, I couldn't recall what I had said that pointed so heavily to my guilt.

There was a busy scramble from the taproom and loud joking as the passengers hurried out. It sounded as though the hot brandy and biscuits had raised everyone's spirits. Linette was talking with her young friend Raoul, who still appeared sullen over his recent misadventure.

Although Marius no longer trusted me, and indeed, violently distrusted me, I noted that he was more than ordinarily interested in each of the passengers as they made their way through the snowdrifts to the coach steps, turning at the last minute to say their farewells to the French countryside they had left behind.

The coachman came waddling around to warn us, 'All papers at the ready, Citizens. The cantons are in confederation with the French Republic, so we may find Swiss mountaineers guarding the high passes ahead between France and Italy. Never know when we will need our papers.'

Several people groaned. I must have groaned silently. If a Frenchman would make trouble over my papers, a Swiss, who might speak German or Italian, would cause more complications. The exact boundaries through these great glacial passes were never precise except in moments of a great battle when they were proclaimed the property of the victor, and few conquerors had dared the conquest of the Alps. Only the armies of ancient Hannibal and of our own General Bonaparte had ever defeated the terrible Alpine passes.

'How many times must we show our papers?' I asked Marius, adding tartly, 'If I were betraying you, I would have correct papers to see me through the journey, wouldn't I?'

'I cannot say what you would have. You are an enigma to me.'

This did not raise my spirits at all and I welcomed Linette's very normal attitude as she came up to the line forming at the coach steps and asked us, 'Are there many borders to check our papers?'

Marius placed his hand on her head and ruffled the hair.

'Don't worry, chérie. We will make do. Your ears are cold.'

'Are there many?'

'The French frontier extends beyond the Mont Cenis Pass. But under the Confederation there may be Swiss guards in the area. Europe is at war, you must remember, and when countries are at war, they love to play with passport papers. We French cannot be too careful, with our enemies so rich with spies.'

I stiffened, and then as Linette and I saw the widow get into the coach, I caught at Marius' arm, drawing him back out of hearing of the others.

'Think what you will, Captain, but Linette and I were suspicious of that woman and I tried to question her, to make her think I was a conspirator. Perhaps I played my role too well. But one thing I did discover. She calls her dead husband "Louis". '

Marius frowned. He and Linette exchanged glances with raised eyebrows. Linette spoke for both of them. 'But it was Gaston. I'm certain. She said he might get warped up on the roof of the coach when the rain was so heavy.'

This time, whatever his intentions, Marius could not help laughing, as I did.

'Yes,' he agreed. 'It was certainly Gaston and not Louis who was going to "get warped". '

I made no further effort to defend myself. It was obvious that he was in two minds about me. I gave him credit for wanting to believe me, but the hazards around him and around Linette had been so great, it was small wonder he could not place full trust in me.

We were the last to get into the coach, and I suggested coolly that Linette might want to talk to her father for a while, and that we would trade seats. She was pleased to do so, but a little puzzled, too. As for me, I no sooner sat down in the corner near the now closed coach door when I became aware of a pair of eyes fixed upon me with deadly intensity. They belonged to young Raoul, across the coach, and feeling sorry for the entire affair, I smiled at him. To my surprise, his glare subsided into a leer. He sat there doing things with his eyes which I daresay he fancied as highly sensual and sure to arouse all my baser emotions. They only gave me a strong desire to laugh at him, which he would never have forgiven.

During those first few minutes, he was not the only one who glanced at me in surprise. The other passengers had been prepared by Marius to see me come forth in Sister Magdalen's garments. Of course, one person among them, or on the box of the coach, knew I could not change to that habit and coif.

The coach rattled, pulled, and jolted us along, ever higher above the passes and the emerald green slopes that appeared like caps on carved granite. We were all cold, though everyone was bundled in both greatcoats and travel cloaks. My own feet felt numb and I tried to exercise them as best I could while Linette, apparently following her earlier suspicions, made small talk with the widow Lallequin. The woman was on her guard, however, and huddled there with her veil lowered over her face and shoulders while she shivered.

Linette gave up presently and sat watching the wall of snow drop away beyond the road, revealing a deep crevasse bordering my side of the coach. I studied this huge blue-white space, uneasily recalling all the horrifying tales of coaches like ours that tumbled off into space, the passengers never heard of again. Linette spoke to me twice in a low, conversational tone before I understood her.

'Where else? I am a French citizen, after all.'

'After Milano, will you return to France?'

'Yes, but will you marry that man? The one we left in Lyon?'

At the far corner of my vision I saw Marius Redon's head turn abruptly. He was watching me, waiting for my answer. I would not yield to temptation and let him see that I was aware of him. I shrugged.

'Who can say? That is all in the future.'

I was vaguely aware that others glanced at me too. They must think me a very modern nun, indeed! A one-time Sister of Mercy who now talked of marrying one man while travelling in company with another man and a boy. Whatever Marius thought he looked away again, and settled into his corner, closing his eyes, as I could not resist seeing out of the periphery of my own vision. But Raoul, my dubious young admirer, probably decided he might pursue his previous dalliance with me. There was too much majesty in the view from the coach window, however, for me to trouble over young Raoul.

In bright, piercing sunlight, we crossed what appeared to be a breathtaking bridge of snow between two crevasses, and most of us held our breath until we reached the comparative safety of a snow-covered road walled in between great drifts of snow. These drifts seemed to be superimposed over blue ice. It was darker now, and we were partially cut off from the sun by the westerly wall of ice. Shortly afterward, the team was reined in and we came to a halt with nothing in sight through the window but a high, cold, blue sky and snow everywhere.

The door was opened and we were invited to descend. For the first time in many days, we saw the red and blue uniform of one of the French frontier units. The small, stern-faced officer was behind the coachman and busy postilion. Like so many of our revolutionary soldiers, he took his tasks with the utmost seriousness. In general, this attitude had proved remarkably fortunate for my country.

We began to descend blindly, at least every passenger was blind except the bride and groom and Captain Marius Redon. It was obvious to me that these three were used to travelling in this blinding glare. I had not looked at Marius yet, but I was aware that the rosy-cheeked bride and her devoted groom had watched the scene of our arrival with hooded eyes. This seemed to serve them in good stead now. They left the coach and stood remarking on the fantastic scene with great ease.

Linette and I blinked while descending with the aid of the coachman and Marius, although my imagination told me that Marius' hand on my elbow threatened to burn through to my very bone, with his hatred of me.

We ignored each other so pointedly that the widow Lallequin whispered to me. 'My dear, you must not let the night fall upon your anger. If you have quarrelled with the Captain, you must kiss and make it up before you sleep, or you will regret it as I regretted many a quarrel with my poor Gaston.' She glanced up at the rooftop of the coach.

So, I thought, Louis had reverted to Gaston!

Everyone milled around in the snow. Eventually, and with squinting eyes, we all made out the little house beyond our coach, built against the mountain-side, although it appeared to me that there was little of the Alps left for us to climb. We certainly were near the peaks by this time.

The French officer gave instructions to the coachman who nodded his tousled grey head and came back to us.

'You are now within a little more than a league of the Mont Cenis Post House, but certain formalities must be dealt with. You will follow me, in line.

Beginning with the Citizeness Lallequin, then the Signore and Signora Albert Adorni, then the young Citizen Raoul de Vaud and after that, the Captain's lady, and the young Citizen Léon Trouville. Am I understood?'

I was surprised when Marius ignored him and strode past him, past the French officer, and into the little house which was evidently large enough to hold two low-ceilinged floors and approximately six rooms. I had no doubt one of those rooms was a jail cell with few amenities. Linette and the others stared after Marius, wondering. I prayed that he would straighten out my own passport difficulties while he was in that house talking with his fellow officers. Surely, no matter what he felt, he would not abandon me at this juncture!

Unfortunately, the Captain's calm assumption of command placed Linette and me in the bad books of our fellow passengers. Linette felt it too, and suggested that we walk about and exercise our limbs after the long trip in one position. I followed her advice. I was too nervous and too cold to stand still. The other passengers had filed along in the wake of the captain.

I was not certain that I had been wise to follow Linette when she took me beyond the post, into the narrow coach road where we reached a breath-taking view of what lay ahead. A world of sparkling white was beautiful in prospect, but it also revealed coming horrors. The left border of the road itself had no protective cliffs and ice deposits, no snowy walls that I could make out. The view was a night-mare drop to a world so far below it was impossible to make out the end of that fall.

'It's horrid, isn't it?' Linette remarked interes-tedly. 'One of the team could slip on a sliver of ice in the roadway, or the coachman could drink a drop too much and give the wrong tug – or whatever he does – to the reins, and see where we would land.'

I shuddered. 'Do come away.' As the stern little officer came out of the wooden Alpine chalet, I added, 'I'm almost as nervous of that interview with the officers. If they don't accept my word and description—'

'Don't say it! Don't think it! Oh, Clare, they want you . . . us – now.'

'They want me,' I said, seeing the signals in front of the chalet. 'You are perfectly safe, dear.'

Nevertheless, her nervous grip on my fingers left bruises that I could well understand. And whether her concern was for herself or for me, I loved her for her companionship. The other passengers seemed to have vanished, which was understandable. Smoke poured out of the chimneys of the little Alpine house. They must be inside getting warm.

Linette and I walked into the building. Despite its exterior, I expected to find an official looking interior, bare, chilling, and formal, but it was obvious that this had been one of those inns among the great Alpine passes whose original owner hoped to profit by the grand tours of the eighteenth century in which so many prosperous young English milords travelled through France, over Mont Cenis and down into the Italian provinces. These had been cut off first by the French Revolution and then by the wars which the rest of Europe had initiated against our new Republic. Of late, an inn-keeper might have done better, with the constant passage of the mail coaches and military couriers.

We walked into a central chamber that seemed excessively warm after the icy brilliance outside. Everyone was watching us as we entered, although our group was presumably warming its backsides against a crackling fire. Where they got the great logs whose sap provided the crackle, I could not imagine, as trees were scarce at this height, but the word had been rapidly bruited about Paris that General Bonaparte always got what he set out to get, and comfort for his troops was one of those requirements. The odours of cooking were savoury, to say the least, but as no one at the fire was either eating or drinking, I knew that what we smelled was the early afternoon dinner of the officers stationed here.

Marius came out of some room at the rear of the building and brought Linette and me back to a small office where an officer in the old-fashioned black plumed hat of our Revolutionary Convention still held sway, not yet having been issued the new uniform. A tall, gaunt man, he intimidated us at once, until I saw that Marius' papers seemed to have a magic effect.

'Citizeness, I am informed by the Représentative en Mission here, Captain Redon, that you are a part of his mission, that you are, in fact, Sister Magdalen Marie Pelletier, a loyal nun who has sworn allegiance to the Republic and our new Constitution.' He kept looking from the papers in his hand to me, obviously checking my description.

Not liking to lie so directly, I said instead, 'My habit has been stolen between Lyon and our last post stop, Citizen.'

'Lieutenant,' the man in the plumes corrected me, then looked at Marius. 'You insist that the widow is not what she appears?'

'I do not insist, Lieutenant, I suggest. It is a suspicion first expressed by Sister Magdalen . . .'

'And me,' Linette put in.

The officer ignored this. He was clearly not fond of children or nuns. He got up, went to a door behind his desk and to my surprise, a cold, grim-looking guardroom was beyond. Two young soldiers in the garbled, piecemeal uniform worn in the

205

Italian campaign, came to order. The officer directed them to bring in the widow Lallequin.

'And her coffin should be examined,' Marius suggested.

The two young soldiers were wide-eyed at this news, but the officer never batted an eye. 'And her coffin, naturally.' Almost as an afterthought, he asked, 'Where might the coffin be?'

Marius explained that it was on the roof of the coach, securely tied, and leaving little room for the usual assortment of luggage. While one of the soldiers went out to check the coffin, the other fetched in the widow, who came lamenting all the way. She was ordered to throw off her veils. Marius and the Lieutenant walked around her, studying her. Then the lieutenant reached over and to my horror, snatched off her bonnet. Her crisp grey curls came with it. Beneath was shorn, pale-blond hair and a head that looked clearly masculine now.

The imposter had stopped complaining, and I felt sorry for him. I suspect Linette shared my pity.

The eyes, curiously light, were keener than I had suspected. Marius asked quietly, 'Were you sent to kill the child?'

The widow opened his mouth and swiped his tongue over his teeth nervously, but it would have been impossible to feign the astonishment that he clearly revealed.

'No! To kill a child? No. I am a loyal soldier. The Emperor does not employ assassins to do his work.'

The Lieutenant and Marius exchanged glances.

'Good God!' Marius dismissed the matter in disgust. 'He is only an Austrian. An imperial spy! The Alps are full of them. That is precisely why you are here, Lieutenant.'

The Lieutenant did not like Marius' attitude. 'Very true, but we do not dismiss spies as lightly as you

Représentatives en Mission, Captain, merely because you carry the signature of the First Consul. Is your private matter concerning the child attended to?' He did not add that he hoped so, but the inference was clear. 'Then I wish you a good trip.'

Marius thanked him, took Linette's arm and mine, and walked out with us. We passed the coachman and the soldier who had taken down the coffin and were prising out the pegs. The Lieutenant and his prisoner came out to the public room to watch.

'Sand!' one of them called out.

'What will happen to the spy?' I asked Marius as we started for the coach.

'If our relations with the Austrian Empire are stable at the moment, he will be held for the returning coach to Lyon and sent down as a prisoner. If not – ' His silence was significant. 'It's a very uncertain life. Poor devil!'

I shivered and asked no more particulars.

Nor did I think too much about the spy afterward, for we shortly came upon our own little life and death drama.

We had been so shaken by the removal of the chatty little 'widow' from our midst that even Marius got into the coach after us without a word to the coachman or the postilion. He was usually very careful to take note of everything, but now, tired and still tense, he settled back into the seat, was stabbed in the back by a cheese, and angrily jerked out the hard chunk from the coach's leather pocket behind him. Lowering the window, he hurled it out into the snowbank.

'Oh, Albert!' the chubby-cheeked bride complained. 'You remember when we stopped so suddenly? You dropped our cheese into that pocket for safekeeping. That was our own cheese.'

Marius glowered at them and Albert apparently felt it too risky to press the matter. The coach started up with its usual disregard of bone and limb, and I looked anxiously out the window, knowing we were about to pass along a mountain ledge so narrow I felt sure even a walking traveller could not pass our coach with safety. On Marius' side of the coach a sheer, snow-covered wall presented our only protection, and it shut out the fast-sinking sun. On my side was nothing. The wheels and the horses' hooves spun slivers of ice and snow over into the abyss.

Even the young people, Linette and Raoul de Vaud, were impressed. Raoul had settled himself opposite me, placing his feet so that they would touch mine, and seeming to pursue my feet in an annoying way until an ominous throat-clearing sound from Marius made the boy jump guiltily and stare out the window, where the view was not inclined to soothe him.

With the exception of Marius, everyone in the coach stopped whispering about the fate of our late fellow passenger, and shifted toward the abyss side of the coach to stare at the incredible view and to wonder how far it must be to the distant bluish peak beyond the abyss. It was a horrid moment for the coach to pull up short. Most of us screamed. We held tightly to anything that looked more secure than we felt.

We sat scarcely breathing, scarcely daring to roll our eyes to see whether the postilion slipped and tumbled over the edge as he snaked his way along to the door, opened it, and squeezed his head in to ask hoarsely,

'Captain! Could we ask your help for a little problem ahead?'

'No!' I cried without thinking. 'You will be in danger of – ' Everyone looked at me and then at Marius, who coloured a little. I had obviously insulted the pride of this maddening man.

Marius got up and stepped over our feet, taking care not to rattle the coach or the rest of us, who were petrified with fear. At the door he asked, 'What has happened?'

'Seems to be a frozen body on the trail. Military man, Captain, and you being the only military man aboard . . . '

'Very well, stand aside.' He moved easily, with great care, stepping down into the snow that had been cast upon the edge of the trail by the horses' hooves. With my heart in my mouth, I kept the door open slightly to watch the procedure. I was thankful that Marius was light-footed. He moved rapidly toward the horses. The little postilion had gone to the boot of the coach and now he started back, following Marius' steps very close against the coach. He passed me without realising the coach door was not tightly closed.

'I can't see!' Raoul cried. 'What is happening?'

Linette pushed against me frantically. 'I don't like it, Clare, what is Marius about?'

But I was too busy watching the postilion move more and more rapidly until he was just behind Marius. I saw the surprising muscular spread between the little man's shoulders as he raised his hands to Marius' back, and I opened my mouth to scream. Then it all happened.

CHAPTER FOURTEEN

MARIUS was pinned between the lead horse of the team and the edge of the great crevasse. I screamed a warning. He seized the harness, handling the horse with that strength and command he had shown when he saved me from the skittish mare drawing the tumbrel. He seemed to dissolve into the flank of the horse for an instant as the postilion made his terrible push forward. The postilion's propulsion carried him past Marius in that narrow space, and the snow and ice shaved away, taking with it his footing. He hurtled over the edge and into nightmare space.

Behind me, Linette was crying out, 'What happened? Let me see . . .'

Her cry was echoed by the others, who pushed against me in what I took to be panic and curiosity, so that the coach door flew open and I clung half to the door latch, half to the wall of the coach, with nothing beneath me but the enormity of space.

'Stop it!' Linette cried over and over. 'You are pushing us.'

I knew the danger of struggling to find a foothold. I think I must have been dazed with fear, but I held on tightly. Linette reached for me but I knew her strength was too feeble to save me. And then, from nowhere, a hand reached for me and prised my fingers away from the latch, lifting me onto the snowy edge of the trail, pressed tight against his body.

I looked at Marius Redon, trying to express my gratitude, but he dismissed this with the cool remark, 'Now we are quits.' We had saved each other's lives and were still no closer than we had been when he hated and mistrusted me. With one hand he slammed the coach door shut, while the other arm held me. He said to Linette, 'Hold tight, soldier! Don't let anyone in there touch you.'

Linette's voice called with forced calm, 'Yes, Captain! Tight it is!'

Marius said to me then, 'Step only where I step, and don't look down. Or up, if it comes to that.'

'Why not l-look up?'

'Because wolves prowl these passes. Hungry wolves. They would enjoy a slice of our horses. Or of you.'

I ignored that, with an effort. He let me go and I obeyed, taking slow strides deep into the snowy drift where his boots had made imprints. We reached the head of the coach. I had not looked down once. Now, I saw the old coachman, obviously frightened, but with steady hands for the team. He called down to us in querulous terror, 'I knew nothing. I swear it. Nothing, Monsieur Captain.'

Marius ignored this. He strode ahead with me and with his boot-toe touched the dark thing half-buried in the snow. 'I thought as much.' There was nothing beneath the blue military cape. But how long had it been there? It couldn't have been placed by the murderous postilion, for it was half-covered with snow, and we had not had snow during the day. The plan must have been worked out with more than the postilion involved. Someone ahead of us.

To me Marius said, 'The inn is around the cliff ahead. Can you sit up there with the coachman?'

Before I could answer, he boosted me up beside the old man, who looked affronted to see a female so close to his sacred box, but he knew his job and took his cue from Marius. The latter, meanwhile, had swung into the postilion's saddle and was leading the skittish team ahead. Not one person had looked over into the crevasse after the wretched man. Was he still falling? Had he struck a ledge on the way down?

Beyond the crevasse, the last broken rays of a now-clouded sun illuminated a little edge of trees. There were trees and even a frozen waterfall in view along the opposite granite wall as we reached the cliff that Marius had pointed out. The inn lay ahead in a little pass with an open view both to the east and the west. There were a number of people milling about outside the inn, which was two and a half storeys of half-timbered, medieval-looking construction, astonishing at this altitude. On the near side was a curious, one-storey structure of wood and stone to which flurries of snow, driven by the wind, clung like paint. From the sounds behind those walls, I guessed this building housed the livestock, the horses for the teams, and the mules for the dangerous descent to the Italian plains.

Several of those figures from the inn, black against the snow, came striding toward us. I was sure my feet and my wet, snow-crusted skirts had frozen fast, and the smoke pouring out of the inn's chimneys suggested heavenly warmth to me. I was no longer worried about Marius. He had certainly overcome every obstacle thrust in his way and every attempt to stop him or Linette. I was positive nothing would stop him now.

Meanwhile, we drew up before the inn, where a wide, level area had been kept almost clear of snow. At the far end of this open area was a barrier of wood and stone protecting us and the livestock from the crevasse, whose far side was breathtaking in the splendour of that frozen waterfall halfway down the grim wall. There were unexpected little pockets of trees across the abyss that reduced the awful grandeur of those cliffs and gave them a touch I found almost domestic.

Although I tried not to do so, I glanced in Marius' direction, wondering as he dismounted if he would help me down. Whether he would have done so, I had no way of knowing. A big man came up to the coach, reached for me, and lifted me down, kissing me noisily on the cheek. It was Paul. I had instinctively turned my head when he leaned toward my face, but he seemed quite unable to comprehend my coldness.

'I am determined not to lay any blame on you, Clare, for abandoning me in Lyon. But one day I shall pay that wretch who forced you to this. Small wonder the princess has no very high opinion of him.'

'How did you get here before our coach?' I asked flatly. I was aware that Marius, on his way to get Linette, stopped momentarily to hear Paul's answer. It was given with Paul's usual exuberance.

'Ah, that! Simple! I found there had been such a crowd who couldn't get booked onto the Mont Cenis Coach that there was another coach the following morning, I booked myself onto that one. We came to the inn here from that westerly route a league or so south. We were afraid you would be late. The Alpine-Torino Coach leaves here at dawn, and there have been difficulties of late with attacks on the coach teams by starving wolves in the area.'

So it had not been Marius' peculiar sense of humour! And Marius and I had been plodding all around in the snow back beyond that cliff! Either of us, or the team itself, might have been attacked.

Paul chided me, 'That was a very unkind thing you did back in Lyon, my dear, but I daresay we can thank that rascal of a captain for the idea. He forced you, I have no doubt!'

'Oh, Paul, don't be so incredibly stupid!'

This hurt his feelings, and I was sorry for it, but it was too much to have to put up with his nonsense when a part of me was also wondering whether he might still be the agent of the principessa.

'Nevertheless,' he agreed, forgiving me in what I now concede was a generous way, 'I know you obeyed the rascal with the best intentions in the world. You know that my patroness, the princess, or members of her family, wished you to hurry the child to Italy. I often wonder what Redon actually intends to do once he reaches Milano. Will he fight the princess in the courts? He seems remarkably improved in health. I was quite astonished to see him there, riding like a postilion. What possessed him to do it?'

'The postilion tried to murder him,' I said, and paid no further attention to Paul's expressions of horror or his natural curiosity.

Everyone was headed toward the inn by this time, and as I was freezing, I hurried Paul along as close behind Marius and Linette as I could walk with my feet soggy in my snow-filled shoes, and my ankles lashed by the regular beat of my heavy skirts. By the time we reached the public room and the tapster's bar across one corner of the room, the place seemed to be swarming with people, most of whom I assumed were waiting to take the Alpine-Torino Coach on the morrow.

Paul left me to go to the taproom to fetch me a warming drink, remarking, 'Naturally, my affianced bride cannot be seen close to the bar.' Unfortunately, the roaring fireplace was near the taproom. I wanted to argue the point with Paul but he was already gone.

Furious with the world, I moved to a corner

behind several gossiping men in wool jerkins, breeches and stockings. These men appeared to be guides who spoke in a wholly incomprehensible dialect which was probably German-Swiss.

Still shaky from the death of the postilion and the near death of Marius, I took the hem of my skirt and began to press it between my hands, squeezing out a river of water. Women across the room stared at me and then talked among themselves. The pink-cheeked bride smiled at me but then pinched her husband's arm as if to draw his attention to me. I really did not care. I went back to wringing out my skirt when a shadow came between me and the room. I was so delighted to see Marius Redon that I lost my tongue and uttered the unromantic, 'You!'

He still looked forbidding, but that may have been concern for all the problems that faced him.

'Come along,' he ordered me. 'We shall be a sorry group to present tonight. You need wringing out.'

'Present to whom?' I asked, plodding along, wet and bedraggled, a sad contrast to him. He managed to look dashing and only slightly windblown. It was grossly unfair.

'I am expecting someone,' he explained briefly. 'The man I came to meet.'

This was news, indeed! 'But I thought we were to go on to Milano.'

'Properly escorted. However, he is late.'

I thought of the principessa. 'Could something have happened to your friend?'

He did not answer. His silence seemed an affirmative. We came into a private parlour now, and as I saw Linette, I felt absurdly sentimental, remembering the private parlours and public coaches we three had shared. Linette had already changed into some local boy's garments complete with a sheepskin

216

jerkin and was examining a full, dark, stuff skirt. I had a horrid premonition this unbecoming thing was for me, but I was too wet and cold to argue.

Marius left me with Linette, who poured out water into an ancient pewter bowl and stood before the small fire in the grate while I washed. When I had changed to the dark green skirt and a close-fitting jacket whose sleeves were a trifle long, I felt for all the world like a tapster's girl. Linette folded back the cuffs of my sleeves and I was at least warm and decently clothed.

'I daresay it isn't a Paris style, but it looks quite charming on you, Clare.'

I thanked her, with a touch of irony for the compliment but at least I was warm and dry. Had I relied upon my betrothed, I might now be warm inside but frozen outside. Marius came in while I was still fastening the innumerable buttons on my jacket. He had not removed the cloak he wore over his greatcoat, and he carried two hooded cloaks over one arm. He tossed one to Linette, who grinned, asked no questions, and threw it around her shoulders. The other he placed around me but I did not seem to be dressing quickly enough, and he buttoned up my jacket with an efficiency that caused me a twinge of jealousy. Had he aided ladies in this way very often?

After what I considered far too long a silence, I felt entitled to ask, 'Are we leaving at once?'

'At once. Out there is a room full of the old harridan's friends, if not her relatives. Are you willing?'

He trusted me. Thank God, he had not just escaped with Linette and left me behind!

'Of course I am willing,' I said.

He had finished the last button of my jacket, under my chin, and was removing his hands as I looked up. Neither of us expected or was prepared

217

for that moment. He drew me to him by the collars of my cloak and I kissed him. Or he kissed me. I had been confused by the swiftness of his orders and the military promptness with which he carried them out. And now, I was in his arms, and in that brief time that we kissed, I remained confused but felt a sensation of delight so exquisite it was painful.

Smiling, he released the collars of my cloak. It was the first time he had looked cheerful in hours, I thought.

'Well, it seems we have survived the eighteenth century together. I confess a few weeks ago I never thought to survive anything. I feel lucky tonight.'

A great many people I had known had not survived the century's end. They would not see the bright new century tomorrow morning, as we would. But Marius had forgiven me, and that was everything. He called to Linette, 'Come, soldier! On the last night of the old year, let's get the start on our enemies.'

'Back passage as usual?' Linette asked happily.

'How well she understands conspiracies!' Marius remarked to me. Linette, staring behind him at the door, suddenly uttered a peculiar sound between a gasp and a scream, and he turned to her, startled.

Paul Vallier, huge and menacing, loomed behind Marius with a pistol barrel clearly visible in his hand. Everything happened at once, and so rapidly I saw only the blur of Paul's hand as the blow was struck. At the moment that Linette and I cried out, Marius fell. He had put out his hands in an instinctive reaction to protect himself, and his palms took the hardest of the blow as he struck the floor. He lay there, the right half of his face visible and looking like marble. Like death.

Rushing to kneel beside him, not knowing whether he was unconscious or dead, I ignored Paul and screamed to Linette, 'Water, Linette! The pitcher beside you—'

I got no further. Paul lifted me over Marius' body with his left arm. His right hand still had the big pistol. I yelled at Paul, 'Are you mad? Don't touch me! I warn you—' The complete innocence of his troubled expression was baffling as he dragged me toward the door.

'Clare, my child, the fellow is a rogue and a liar. I daresay, an abductor as well. I haven't killed him. Don't let him concern you. We have no time to lose. His friends may reach here at any minute.'

I cried, 'Linette! Run for help! Linette!' Then I saw the child struggling madly in the arms of Albert, the clumsy bridegroom who had shared our coach. He had one hand over her mouth and she was trying to bite him. The round-cheeked bride was in the doorway, watching us impatiently.

'We've no time. Grandmama should meet us before midnight. Hurry!'

I hung back, making every possible difficulty. I could see that blood had matted in Marius' hair, and trickled over his right temple. The sight panicked me and I begged Paul, 'Please, please let me help him. Then I will go, if you only let me . . .'

'Forgive me,' he said in that odious, implacable way of his that reminded me of the times when I was a girl and had supposed it was a man's place to be all-knowing. 'You will thank me in the end. The principessa is to meet us. These are her grandchildren. They have been of great help. She is a shrewd woman. She had stationed agents on all Alpine Coaches leaving Lyon that day and the next. Remarkable female!'

'Murderess! Abductor! That is what she is,' I managed to get out as we reached the passage. I tried to be as loud as possible, hoping someone would hear, someone who might be on Marius' side in this terrible vendetta. But the principessa's grandchildren, the bride and bridegroom, pushed me along, and like Linette, I had no chance to escape or even to cause enough annoyance so that we would disturb those travellers gathered in the public room. I was sure I saw a shining bayonet in that room, belonging to one of the National Guardsmen we were likely to see anywhere in France these days, but it was obvious he was too busy drinking to hear me.

I tried to cry out again. This time the bride gave me such a clout over the ear that my head rang for minutes afterward. Paul lifted me, and I found myself helpless, immovable in that now revolting embrace.

Paul carried me out through a door into the crisp, glittering night. Linette and I were dropped into a tumbrel, landing painfully on our elbows and knees, although I will do Paul the justice of admitting he exclaimed angrily at the violence done to us.

'Easy, there! Name of God, Monsieur Alberto, that is my betrothed, and the child is Her Highness' great-granddaughter.'

I did not like the sound of the bride's nasty laugh but I was busy trying to revive Linette, who was dazed and looked frighteningly pale. As Linette clung to me and I held her, I called to Paul loudly, fiercely, still hoping my voice would reach someone who might help us. 'Paul, they have hurt the girl. Is this what you want? You must help us. *Please . . . help us!*'

Paul, on the coachman's box, turned to look back down at me. He appeared concerned but turned back to watch the narrow road. Then Albert struck me under the jaw with his clenched fist. It was a sensation I had never known before, and certainly never hope to feel again. I lost consciousness, but only briefly, I think. I remember that I did not

220

even feel the icy cold of the night. I opened my eyes to see a heaven full of stars. My chin was frightfully sore, my jaw numb, but Linette leaned over me, looking relieved.

With great difficulty, I managed to ask, 'Are they real?'

She murmured, 'You're not dead! What do you mean, are they real?'

'The stars.'

'Oh, yes. They're up there. We're nearly at the crossroads where the old harridan's coach is expected.' I saw the detestable Albert squatting in the tumbrel, staring out at the snowy peaks. Then Linette lowered her head over me. She whispered, 'That Vallier, his pistol is in the pocket of his greatcoat. Right pocket.'

I murmured painfully, but I was sure she understood that I had heard. I needed a few minutes longer in which to recover. By the expression in my eyes and a pinch at her hand I let her know that I was planning something important.

I sat up and pulled on Paul's sleeve. 'Paul?'

The reins were wrapped around his knuckles, but he kept them still as he looked back at me. He seemed inordinately pleased at the softening of my tones.

'Good girl! Feeling better, are you? We shall be comfortable very soon. Have you decided to make it up with me?'

I looked hard, though briefly, at Linette. To Paul, I said in my meekest voice, 'You are in the right, of course, my dear. I should have known. But do take me out of here. I ache in every bone.'

'Promise to behave like my own little girl?'

I wrinkled my nose at Linette. It seemed incredible to me now that I had ever been moved by that form of solicitude. 'I promise,' I told him, though the words burned in my mouth.

'Lift her up beside me, and be gentle,' he told the bridegroom, who looked disgusted. Albert tried to touch me, but I got up without his help, and with my head ringing like an alarm bell, I managed to climb up beside Paul. Breathless, I settled there less than a hand's length from the huge pistol in his greatcoat pocket.

'Now,' he promised me, 'You will see that I was right, as your lamented parents always agreed. I knew what was best for you, and you will soon discover I was in the right about my patroness.'

'Of course. Where is she? Heavens! How cold it is!'

I clasped my hands under the cloak Marius had wrapped around me. Marius, whom we had left bleeding upon the floor of the inn. Was he badly hurt? He had survived so much and was so close to his goal.

As my numb, chilled fingers thawed, I thought steadily of that pistol in Paul's pocket.

Behind us the bride and her Albert stirred, and he called, 'There! She swore she would be here waiting, and she *is* here.'

Through the starlight and across the white mountain meadow, I made out another road emptying into our own. I saw coach lamps and then the closed coach in which, I did not doubt, that ancient spider, the principessa, was waiting. Paul had been right. When we reached the crossroads, Albert lifted the blonde woman out of the tumbrel. The two plodded through the wagon ruts made by the coach that had brought Paul to the Mont Cenis Inn. I watched them, thinking, scheming in so devious a manner I scarcely knew myself. Should I try now for that pistol? Did I dare, with my head aching and my absolute conviction that Paul would stupidly let me shoot him before he would let Linette and me run away? I reached for Linette, touched her hand. It was a signal, as I hoped she would understand. I assumed there would be only one ball in the pistol Paul carried, and we had a minimum of half a dozen enemies. It might be used as a threat, but that was all.

Linette nudged me. Everyone was looking to the west across the snowy meadow, but something in her gesture made me look down the mountainside, down our own road, that narrow, winding little shelf on the side of a great wall, that twisted around, sometimes out of sight, then appeared again. And down along one of those shelving ledges, a coach was climbing, a black insect against the white wall on one side and the great abyss on the other. But it would not reach this point in time to prevent whatever the princess intended for us.

The so-called bride and groom had got into the princess' coach and the team was given the signal to move forward until the coach and team were perilously close to the abyss. The horses pawed the snow uneasily as the coachman urged them around until they faced down the ledge trail, but still on an angle toward that enormous drop. As the coach door opened and the bride and groom got out and let down the steps, the Principessa Visconti descended into the wheel tracks where her small, elegant boots would not be inundated with snow. She signalled, and Albert reached for Linette, who came out of the tumbrel screaming, scratching and kicking.

Paul lifted me down. It was important that I lull his suspicions, so I made no struggle, but as they walked Linette and me to the princess' coach, she and I exchanged significant looks. We were both ready for any opportunity.

By the coach lights I saw the old woman looking drier and bonier than ever. She seemed to have shrivelled and yet this only added to her malevolence. She was like a basilisk with only greed and hatred for that child whose great-grandmother had been fortunate enough to be the first wife of the Principe Visconti. Her eyes, watery and pale, gazed upon me with the same fixed indifference that the eyes of a serpent might have shown. She touched my hand with inhumanly dry fingers.

CHAPTER FIFTEEN

'WHAT a sly boots you were, my dear! Our good Paul was to have escorted you on the journey. Instead, you chose that dreadful rogue who should have died for his sins long ago. But no matter. Mount the steps. And my little grandchild after you. You will have an inestimable advantage by making the end of your journey in my well-sprung coach.'

Linette did not move. The bride prodded her, but she would not budge. I said pleasantly, 'Your Highness will, of course, give us the pleasure of your company in your well-sprung coach?'

I did not miss the quick flash of understanding and amusement between the bride and Albert, and was convinced even before the old woman spoke that Linette and I were meant to die in that coach.

'Alas! That pleasure I must forgo, at least for the first section of the journey. I have business at the inn here. We must really see to that rascal who has given us so much trouble, if he is still alive, of course. Mount, girl!'

'A moment, Your Highness. Are you not curious to know the fate of the postilion on the Landsel Coach?'

'My nephew, Alberto here, described the unhappy event. My fault, of course. I was so sure Marius Redon had never been in the cavalry. Only a man who understood horses could have saved himself in that moment. Else one of those hooves would certainly have completed the job.'

'What is all this?' Paul demanded. 'No one has mentioned anything about a postilion.'

'She is planning to murder Linette and me, Paul. And perhaps you as well.'

Instinctively, he moved closer to me. Poor man! So predictable!

'Clare! Name of God! These accusations – tell her how wrong she is, Your Highness. Reassure her.'

Now the princess was on my right, near the coach door, and Paul was on my left, so it was a simple matter to reach into his greatcoat pocket and remove the pistol. Linette, the old campaigner, had been watching me for a signal. She had wriggled out of Albert's clutches and was on the run almost before my move.

Both Alberto and the bride turned and started after her. They seized her, swung her around in a way that made her cry out as they caught her between them.

I shouted, 'Stop! Don't move!'

They obeyed on the instant. The pistol was much bigger and heavier than I had expected it to be, but it was clear they didn't trust such a weapon in my inexperienced hands. There was always a possibility I would panic and shoot. Paul was spellbound and kept muttering, 'Good God, Clare! Are you mad? Here, let me take that before you hurt yourself.'

But I had worked it all out and was ready when the bride gave her hideous, cutting laugh. 'Only one ball in that pistol. There are many of us and only one of you.'

The snowy meadow seemed to loom above us where we stood on the ledge trail, and I thought, if only Linette could have got up there, above the ledge, to the safety of the meadow! Paul reached for the pistol, but I jerked away.

'It is quite true, I can shoot only one person,'

226

I said loudly, attempting an ease and confidence I was far from feeling. 'But I choose to shoot Her Highness. And without Her Highness, your hopes of the Visconti fortune are quite, quite dead.'

That stopped them. Linette giggled hysterically.

'Now, see here, Clare, you are not yourself,' Paul began. 'Give me that pistol and let the princess tell you her plans.'

'Don't touch me, Paul! You have been fool enough to believe—'

Behind me, something very like a series of ropes wound itself around my throat, my waist, and then, as I screamed and heard the sound echoed by Linette, one of those rope hands moved away from my throat and a second later, that hand hammered down upon my wrist. The pain was excruciating and instinctively my fingers squeezed the trigger. The heavy pistol dropped into the snow.

In the agony of pain to my wrist I heard behind me the detestable voice of the principessa's dark, slimy little agent, Ridetti. 'She had fangs, our pretty Clare! What a pity she had so little taste for my brandied cake! This might have been unnecessary.'

In spite of my pain I was so angry, so frustrated, I screamed, 'Paul! Do you not see they mean to murder us? If you do nothing else in life, please save Linette!'

'Now, see here . . .' Paul tried to interfere, but far too late. He reached out to force Ridetti's hands from me. 'Take your hands from her, you little beast!' But the man pulled from his jerkin a very serviceable gun, much smaller than Paul's, and ordered Paul, 'Into the coach!'

Astonished, his manhood outraged at being ordered about, Paul started up the steps and vanished inside.

'Now, the brat!'

Alberto gave Linette a push in the small of the

227

back. She nearly fell. I reached out instinctively, kicking the detestable Ridetti, but to no purpose. I could not free myself.

'And now, our clever little Clare.' Ridetti had waited a second or two for instructions from the princess, but the old woman who had been standing so close beside me, said nothing. She stared at the bride and Alberto, as if accusing them of some inadequacy. No one could accuse Ridetti of being inadequate!

I clung to the coach door as he pushed me up the steps. I would not climb. I did everything to delay, but it was no use. I had counted on a dream, that Marius would recover, that the coach climbing the precipitous ledge trail would arrive. Nothing happened. I was thrown into the coach against Linette. Paul was at the opposite window. The ropes that let it down had been sealed. He crashed it with his boot. He reached out then, trying vainly to lower what remained of the window, but the side of the coach had been reinforced.

I looked over his shoulder. The sight appalled me. I was looking down into the abyss, the great glacial valley.

As Ridetti and Alberto started to slam the door on the ledge side, Paul stuck his booted foot in the doorway. I was behind him, reaching out, trying to claw at the two who imprisoned us. One of them hurled his own empty pistol at Paul, and he stumbled back against Linette and me. The door was slammed. Through the window on the ledge side I saw Ridetti throw balls of ice and snow at the horse, and the coach jerked forward, without coachman or postilion.

Behind me, Linette's shaky voice said, 'He's dazed, but he will come around. Clare, can we stop the horses?'

Paul kept muttering, 'How could she do this

fiendish thing? I knew her so well. She lied to me. I would have staked my life on her honour.'

'You *have* staked your life on her honour,' I reminded him harshly. I was trying to get the door open. Ridetti had done something to this door so that it stuck. I heard a sound, a snap like a stick breaking in the cold air outside. A rifle shot! Could it be a signal to stop the princess and her ruffians? The team halted. The coach jerked back and forth.

Linette whispered, 'We're about an arm's length from the edge.'

But I was banging my fists against the window on the ledge side until I finally broke the restraining cords, and I lowered the window. I could see a man above the ledge at a slight distance from us. It was Marius. He stood on the edge of the meadow with a rifle at his feet. And another rifle with a long bayonet in his hands. It was aimed at the coach, a little to the left of me, where Alberto and Ridetti stood. Alberto was groaning heavily. He had been grazed in the forearm by the first rifle. A youth stood beside Marius, aiming at our cutthroat crew with a similar rifle. Had this youth, Raoul de Vaud, come to Marius' rescue?

Marius' face was suddenly illuminated by our flaring coach lights as he moved closer, looking determined and deadly. There was a dark streak on his temple and cheek where the blood had dried, but he seemed in every other way quite in command of the situation.

No one could doubt that he meant it when he ordered Ridetti, who was scrambling to the coachman's box, 'Hold fast to those reins, if you wish to live!'

I forced the door open and got out. Paul, with Linette's arm around him, followed. It was then that Linette cried in astonishment, 'But it's Raoul who helped Marius. Raoul, you are a hero!'

The young man managed not to lose his grip upon his rifle, but one could see he was proud enough to burst. Marius looked down at me. We need say nothing in that moment.

Marius turned to the princess, 'Come forward. You first, Your Highness. I think we had better extract the poison from this little nest of vipers.'

The princess, still standing as she had been when I left her side, raised her head slightly, seemed to catch a glimpse of Marius, and took a small step forward. To everyone's amazement, she collapsed in a tiny heap. Alberto and the bride bent over her. Even I came to see what had happened. It seemed unlike her, I thought, to be so strong in committing all manner of crimes and to faint at the first sign of being found out!

Then the bride screamed. Ridetti, busy pulling up the coach and team, looked back over his shoulders in fright. Marius leaped down to the ledge trail and came toward us with the rifle still at the ready, but like me, he was clearly baffled by the princess' behaviour. The bride moved away and the coachlights flashed upon the old woman's body. I had never seen so much blood. There was a huge, spreading stain across the back of her cloak, just below her lung.

We stood there staring. Then I remembered.

'Name of God!' I cried. 'It must have been when Ridetti seized me. The pistol went off, and she was close beside me.'

The old woman's relations were too stupefied at her condition to regard me with horror, and I scarcely knew what to think of my own involuntary action, except that it had been ghastly, and I wished very much that the old woman had been shot by some other hand. But across her body Marius looked at me with his grave yet reassuring eyes. 'Had you rather she went on?'

230

The bride screamed again. 'She moved!' I recall that for all my regret at having shot a fellow human being, my first thought was that it took a great deal to kill a poisonous viper.

The Principessa Visconti looked up at Marius. It seemed to me a very clear gaze for a dying woman. She almost smiled. 'A fool. I was – a fool – not to guess. He was a weakling. You were – worthy of my steel . . .'

And her eyes closed. The viper was dead.

Marius looked at Paul Vallier. 'Are you fit enough to bind these three?'

'Perfectly fit,' Paul announced in short, clipped tones. Then he was forced to bend a little in his hauteur. ' . . . Er . . . what shall I use?'

'For one thing,' Marius pointed out, 'the coach door was tied with rope. So was the window sash. And you might tear off the hem of the lady's skirt.' He nodded toward the bride, who yelped but need not have concerned herself. Paul would never have committed so improper an act. Linette giggled and I smiled to myself, but caught Marius' eye. Thank heaven, he also smiled.

Raoul de Vaud leaped down among us, managing not to lose his rifle. He seemed curious about Linette, who was not averse to being the centre of his attention. 'I came to your private parlour,' he explained. 'I saw the Captain and revived him. Did I not?'

'You did. You were in every sense a hero, young sir.'

Raoul grinned at Linette. 'I guessed you were a female, you know. I tried to make you say so.'

'You didn't. You couldn't possibly guess.'

'Well, I did! I tried to make you jealous. But – ' He glanced my way and then avoided me as he went on to Linette, 'you aren't pretty, but you've a way about you.'

231

Linette very properly took these remarks as a handsome compliment. Marius and I laughed softly at this development, and while I kept an eye out for Ridetti's movements, Marius examined the old woman. He got up presently, throwing her cloak over her face.

'She is dead. The shot must have been so shattering she did not realise she had been hit. It often happens that way on the battlefield.' He called to Ridetti on the coachman's seat, 'Get that team back out of the way. A coach is coming up the grade.'

Ridetti, terrified of falling over the side, as well he might be, protested but managed to manoeuvre the team skilfully back into the centre of the road, and still further back to the crossroad. Paul, meanwhile, had his bound and moaning prisoners in order, and with some relish, added Ridetti to them. The little man was completely subdued by the death of his patroness and, like Paul, kept glancing at the motionless bundle in the snow.

Paul asked me, 'Are you coming, Clare?'

I tried to be as gentle as possible, but it was no use. He resented any effort of mine to try and soothe his ruffled feelings while still telling the truth. 'Paul, I am not suited to you. I never would be right for you in Geneva among your banking friends. You must go back there and marry a lovely girl with a great deal of money. It will help you to establish yourself.'

'I am established,' he announced so pompously that I bit my lip.

'Of course, of course. I'm very sorry. I will wait for – Linette and – and the others.'

He glanced at Marius, shook his head at my incredible lapse in taste, then shoved his fist into the small of Ridetti's back. The dejected little line went forward to the inn.

Linette walked up to Marius, who kissed her on the cheek. She hugged him and whispered something. He said, 'Naturally.' She grinned, looked at me, and then went after the prisoners, accompanied by the proud Raoul, his rifle ever at the ready. I only hoped no one would back into that bayonet. I started after them, not quite sure where I was wanted, but Marius, standing over the princess' body, reached out and took my wrist and held me there with the rifle under his other arm. I looked askance at the rifle and bayonet. He laughed.

'Yes. I am armed. As a matter of fact, I borrowed them from two National Guardsmen who are snoring away, drunk, at the inn. I don't intend for you to get away again.'

I felt it undiplomatic to mention that each time it was he who sent me away, but there was another important matter, and I broached it now, frankly.

'It was a curious remark the princess made to you as she died. How was she fooled by you?'

He hesitated, rubbed his thumb along my wrist, then moved his hand to my fingers. 'Cold,' he remarked gently, and added in a strange, stern voice, 'I do love you, you know. It may not have seemed so at times. I am not an easy man. Too long in the army, perhaps. But can you love me?'

I wanted to say, 'You are blind if you do not know I loved you that first night and always.' But I forced myself to resist the impulse. I touched his hand to my lips and tried to make my words sound light, easy.

'Captain Redon, who are you?'

'Does it matter to you so very much?'

'No.' I said instinctively, straight out, and he laughed with obvious relief.

'You will soon know, in any case. That coach climbing the ledge trail very probably belongs to Bernardo Visconti, my friend, who campaigned through the Italian Wars with me. He received a spinal injury. He cannot walk, but he has recovered enough to share Linette's guardianship and wrote that he would await our arrival here on the border, in order to bring us into Lombardy.'

Confused, I objected, 'But as Linette's father, you are perfectly capable of acting as her guardian.'

His fingers tightened painfully on mine.

'I am not Linette's father.'

'What?'

'Marius Redon died in the Hôtel Dieu three months ago. Bernardo had corresponded with Sister Magdalen and me, and we agreed to change identities to keep the principessa from gaining control of Linette. It wasn't too difficult. The principessa did not know Redon by sight, and Redon and I resembled each other slightly. He died of lung fever. I had taken a bullet very near the lung. And then, there was Linette herself. She worked as hard to save my life as to save her father. Clare, can you understand that Linette will always be my daughter in every other way but the ties of blood? Can we not be a family, we three?' He smiled, that odd, serious smile of his. 'A family ready provided.' I laughed, delighted at the prospect, trying to cover the break in my voice. 'I wished it. I prayed for it when we came into the private parlour only a few hours ago.'

He glanced up toward the inn.

'From the look of Linette and that young de Vaud, we may have difficulty keeping the child!'

'Nonsense!' I said. 'She is much too young for thoughts of betrothal.' He was amused at my vehemence and I suddenly remembered, 'I do not yet know your name.'

'Since I am officially buried, I think I had best remain Marius Redon. But it is for you to say. Citizeness Clare Dubeque Redon?'

I felt almost light-headed. 'It sounds eminently respectable. What is the alternative?'

'Not nearly so well suited to the new century, which seems to be coming up over those mountain peaks. Before the Revolution, I was Maxime de Mauprat, Comte de St Laure.'

My eyes must have widened. I said after a stunned silence, 'Citizeness Redon suits me much better.' I doubted if my parents would have been pleased to receive a 'comte' in our democratic family!

'It suits me eminently,' he imitated me in a teasing voice. 'And Clare, my darling, one thing more I have been afraid to ask of you.'

'It cannot be worse than a *ci-devant* count in the family!'

He laughed, but his eyes were worried. 'When we have done with Milanese bankers and settled Linette's affairs so that no one may do her harm, I want to return to Paris and gain permission of the First Consul to improve conditions in the Paris hospitals. We spoke of it even before I was on my feet some weeks ago. I think he will appoint me. Will you join me in that too, my darling?'

Curious and providential how our paths had run together, for I too had meant to return to that task!

'You know that I will, that I wish to.'

He kissed me. His rifle came between us and he said, 'I seem to have the most incredible bad luck in trying to kiss you. There is forever some obstacle.'

'Not forever,' I promised him.

THE END

PAT BARR

JADE

A great and sweeping novel of a distant land

A VAST PORTRAYAL OF OLD CHINA, AND A YOUNG ENGLISH WOMAN, TORN BETWEEN TWO CULTURES.

Spanning the last forty years of the old Imperial dynasties, *Jade* sweeps across the land of China, recreating the beauty, the violence, the bigotry, and the last crumblings of a giant civilisation.

From the terrifying massacre of the Christian community in Tientsin, to the ancient and exotic formalities of the Chu household, we follow Alice . . . young, sometimes frightened, often betrayed by the men who love her, but always courageously seeking a place for herself between two totally opposing worlds.

0 552 12281 5   £2.50

CORGI BOOKS

TILLY TROTTER
TILLY TROTTER WED
TILLY TROTTER WIDOWED

Beginning in the reign of the young Queen Victoria, the
three Tilly Trotter novels tell the story of a beautiful girl
growing to womanhood amid hardship and despair.
Pitting her wits against the local Tyneside villagers, who
hate her and accuse her of witchcraft, Tilly's strong
instinct for survival leads her to become, in turn, the
loving mistress of a wealthy man, and then the wife of his
son, travelling to the strange and perilous land of
America.

When her husband is killed, Tilly returns to take posses-
sion of his estate. The villagers prove ever hostile and
suspicious, but Tilly is supported by faithful friends and
warm memories. Life still has much in store for Tilly
Trotter, old loves and enmities providing fresh challenges
to a woman as spirited as ever.

Tilly Trotter	0 552 11737 4	£1.95
Tilly Trotter Wed	0 552 11960 1	£1.95
Tilly Trotter Widowed	0 552 12200 9	£1.95

CORGI BOOKS

DIANE PEARSON
THE SUMMER OF THE
BARSHINSKEYS

'Although the story of the Barshinskeys, which
became our story too, stretched over many summers
and winters, that golden time of 1902 was when our
strange involved relationship began, when our
youthful longing for the exotic took a solid and restless hold upon us . . .'

It is at this enchanted moment that *The Summer of
the Barshinskeys* begins. A beautifully told, compel-
ling story that moves from a small Kentish village to
London, and from war-torn St Petersburg to a
Quaker relief unit in the Volga provinces. It is the
unforgettable story of two families, one English, the
other Russian, who form a lifetime pattern of
friendship, passion, hatred, and love.

'An engrossing saga . . . she evokes rural England at
the turn of the century with her sure and skilful
touch'
Barbara Taylor Bradford

'The Russian section is reminiscent of Pasternak's
Doctor Zhivago, horrifying yet hauntingly beautiful'
New York Tribune

0 552 12641 1   £2.95

CORGI BOOKS

CATHERINE COOKSON

THE BLACK VELVET GOWN

There would be times when Riah Millican came to
regret that her husband had learned to read and
write, and then shared the knowledge with her and
their children. For this was Durham in the 1830s,
when employers regarded the spread of education
with suspicion. Now Seth Millican was dead and
she was a widow with the need to find a home and a
living for herself and her children.

Chance led to Moor House and a scholarly recluse
obsessed with that very book learning that could
open so many doors and yet create so many
problems; especially with her daughter, Biddy, who
was not only bright, but wilful . . .

0 552 12473 7   £2.50

CORGI BOOKS

OTHER FINE NOVELS AVAILABLE FROM CORGI BOOKS

While every effort is made to keep prices low, it is sometimes necessary to increase prices at short notice. Corgi Books reserve the right to show new retail prices on covers which may differ from those previously advertised in the text or elsewhere.

The prices shown below were correct at the time of going to press.